AN U...
A...

BY

LEIGH MICHAELS

MILLS & BOON LIMITED
ETON HOUSE   18-24 PARADISE ROAD
RICHMOND   SURREY   TW9 1SR

First published in Great Britain 1990
by Mills & Boon Limited

© Leigh Michaels 1990

Australian copyright 1990
Philippine copyright 1990
This edition 1990

ISBN 0 263 76834 1

Set in Times Roman 10 on 11¼ pt.
01-9010-56366 C

Made and printed in Great Britain

For Denise and Dave,
for always being there.

CHAPTER ONE

BY THE time Torey Farrell reached the city limits of Springhill, the afternoon sky was almost black and the rain that had been threatening for the last hundred miles had begun to fall. The first few drops were huge, and they splashed against the car with the intensity of falling rocks. Torey's nerves were already stretched by anticipation and the strain of five days on the road, and each time a raindrop smacked into the glass just a few inches from her face she cringed and tightened her grip on the wheel.

Rainstorms had never been one of her favourite things, and as for driving through an unfamiliar city in the midst of a downpour, without a map and without instructions, in search of a house she had never seen—well, it wouldn't have been her first choice of entertainment for an afternoon in early spring, that was certain, Torey told herself with as much humour as she could muster. Her choice would have been a fireside chair, a cup of hot cider, a plate of ginger-snaps, and a book; and the curtains firmly drawn between her and the outside world ...

But, since she couldn't have the fire and the ginger-snaps, the first step was to resign herself to the rain and find Violet Endicott's house. Oh, *why* hadn't she asked for directions?

'Because,' she reminded herself, 'when you were talking to the lawyer you didn't have a glimmer of an idea that you were going to come out here, so you didn't need directions. And besides,' she added with a wry smile, 'everybody on the West Coast told me that towns in Iowa only have three streets—two of which are always called Main and Third—so what could be complicated about getting around?'

Of course, any faith she had put in that myth had died the instant she had reached the city limits of Springhill and looked down into a small, bowl-like valley that was absolutely filled with houses and highways and schools and shopping complexes. It was certainly not Los Angeles, but obviously Springhill did not fit the generally accepted pattern of small Midwestern towns. She wondered how many other things that 'everybody on the West Coast' knew might turn out to be false, as well.

It could have been a pretty sort of town, she thought, but in early March the grey and dingy remnants of the winter's snow still lined the streets and masked the beauty of the simple houses, the spacious lawns, the low skyline. The rain pelted down, pocking the icy clumps and slowly wearing them away, leaving sand and dirt behind.

But surely it can't look like this all the time, she thought. Didn't all the people she knew who had moved to California from the Midwest say that the thing they missed the most was the changing seasons, and especially the beauty of spring? Well, it was almost spring—and it was obvious that it wasn't the sort of springtime she'd been hoping for. She shivered under her thin jacket.

Highway traffic came to an abrupt halt for a red light, and as she waited for it to change Torey noticed a sign that marked the intersecting street as Third Avenue. Perhaps there was a fragment of truth to the myth after all, she thought with a smile, and purely on a whim she turned left as soon as the light changed.

She had the lawyer's telephone number in her handbag, but despite the rain there was a sense of adventure in trying to find her way around by herself first. If she had to, she could always find a telephone and call

Stan Spaulding to rescue her. But she'd rather do it herself.

Besides, this town was going to be her home for a while—a long while, she told herself—and she felt almost a desperate need to get the feel of the place as soon as she could. She wanted to see the house, too—Violet's house—this house she now owned. And she was too impatient to wait around a lawyer's office for him to find time to take her out and show her the property. She could at least drive by it first and look at the outside, couldn't she? There must be some logic to the way streets were named in this town...

In the last five days, as Torey had driven across the country, she had had plenty of time to think about Violet Endicott's house. She had never even seen a photograph of it, and she had never given it any thought, because it had never been important to know where Aunt Violet had lived. But now that Violet was gone and house was Torey's, and now that she had wildly burned her bridges and flung caution to the winds and come halfway across the continent to live in her new possession, her imagination had begun to play tricks on her. The long hours behind the steering-wheel had given her nothing but time to think, and she had spent those hours conjuring up everything from a marble-encased castle in the air to the lowliest tar-paper shack.

'Six hundred, Belle Vista,' she recited stoutly to herself. 'Does that sound like a proper address for a tar-paper shack?'

But the other half of her brain, the uncooperative part, reminded her of an inner-city slum she'd once heard of that was called Starlite Woods, and added that Belle Vista only indicated that the view from the house would be pleasant, and promised nothing about the appearance of the structure itself.

'Oh, stop it,' she told herself firmly. 'You're getting nervous enough to fly.'

A driver who had stopped in the next lane at a traffic light gave her general directions, and she found herself in a residential neighbourhood where large houses sat at prim distances from each other and well back from the traffic. She looked hopefully at the street signs, but it wasn't Belle Vista Avenue. Well, she told herself philosophically, she couldn't have expected that Violet would live in a neighbourhood like this.

Here there were even fewer people walking, and most of them were scurrying for shelter, certainly not interested in being hailed and asked for directions. At a corner, however, a young woman with a little girl beside her was waiting to cross, and Torey wound her window down and pulled as close to the kerb as she could.

She saw the young woman's gaze flick over the old station-wagon, loaded almost to the roof with boxes and bags, as she asked her question. It was a curious glance, as if the woman was wondering what that sort of vehicle was doing in this neighbourhood, but her voice didn't betray her inquisitiveness. 'Belle Vista? It's just two blocks east, but you have to go clear down to Main to find a through street because the rest are culs-de-sac. Which block are you looking for?'

'The house is number six hundred.'

'Six... That's Violet Endicott's house.' Now there was no doubt of the lively curiosity in the young woman's face; her eyes were practically sparkling with it.

Torey nodded.

'But surely——' Then the young woman seemed to think better of it, and she began to give the most precise directions Torey had ever received. When Torey drove off a couple of minutes later, she looked back to see the young woman still standing on the corner, one hand deep in the pocket of her raincoat, the other holding the child's, and looking thoughtfully down the street after the car, as if studying the California licence-plate.

You might as well get used to it, Torey told herself. Don't be fooled by the bustle; Springhill is still obviously a very small town, and everyone is going to know everyone else's business or die trying to find it out. It's just one of the things you'll have to adjust to if you're going to live here.

And she was going to stay; she had made up her mind about that. She was going to be successful. She was not going to go back to Los Angeles in defeat. Springhill was the best opportunity she was ever likely to have, and she owed Aunt Violet a debt of gratitude that could never be repaid.

She took her right hand off the steering-wheel and flexed it, only half conscious of the action, exercising each finger separately as if she had just finished a long session of drawing. She was depending on that right hand now.

As if you haven't always depended on it, she told herself a bit sharply. This is no different, really. You're just going to draw something different now, that's all. You're going to do what you've always dreamed of doing—and you're going to do it well.

Turn left on Main Street, the young woman had said. Two blocks and another left, and she was on Belle Vista. Six more blocks and she would be there...

The houses were fairly close to the street, but that was deceptive, Torey soon realised, because Belle Vista itself was a divided street, two narrow lanes separated by an expanse of grass that was just beginning to show the hazy green of spring. It was like having a park the length of the street just outside the front door of each house. Here and there playground equipment had been set up, and sandboxes awaited the coming of warmer weather. At regular intervals there were old-fashioned street lights, wrought-iron poles topped with white glass globes. Some of them had already sensed the coming darkness and had turned themselves on. It was a pleasant, old, quiet neighbourhood, and Torey breathed a soft sigh of relief. She could work here. She could be happy here.

She had a bit of trouble spotting number six hundred, Belle Vista; it was on a corner and there were three huge old oak trees in front of it. The bushes and shrubs that lined the lawn were overgrown and badly in need of trimming. The house itself was big and white and almost square, a turn-of-the-century structure as solid and practical as the merchants who must have built this entire neighbourhood. It was taller than most of the surrounding buildings, its gambrel roof sheltering three full floors. On the side was a *porte cochère*; in front was a wide, pillared veranda on the ground floor with a balcony above. Here and there the gingerbread trim sagged a bit, but it was all still there.

And in front of the house, almost blocking the narrow traffic lane, was a removal van, its cargo doors open and a ramp extended to the lawn.

The car's brakes squealed in protest as Torey stamped her foot. 'That's my house,' she announced to the world at large. 'And what the hell someone is doing moving into my house, I'd certainly like to know!'

There was no possibility of a mistake; the removal van certainly belonged to number six hundred. The front door of the house stood wide open, and as she watched two burly removal men carried a white leather couch off the van and up the steps to the front veranda. The rain had stopped for the moment, and they were obviously in a hurry.

It was a difficult manoeuvre to steer her car around the van and into the narrow driveway, which had been built for the vehicles of a much earlier day. Torey extricated herself from the tightly packed car, slammed the door and burst across the lawn and up the steps to confront the removal men, who were stamping back across the veranda towards the van. 'Who's in charge here?' she demanded.

One of them jerked his head towards the interior of the house, and Torey stepped across the threshold and into her house.

It was cold and dismal inside; the light in the hallway was on, but the single dim bulb succeeded only in casting shadows across the parquet floor. In other circumstances Torey would have stopped to give the intricate pattern of inlaid wood the admiration it deserved, but today she was too anxious to pay attention.

Her running-shoes didn't make a sound on the parquet, and for a moment there was no other noise anywhere in the house. She stood absolutely still for a while, wondering if she should call out or just start searching from room to room, and then a man's voice spoke from her left, beyond an open doorway formed by glass-doored bookcases and two carved oak posts.

'Marsh, I still say this is not a good idea,' he said.

You shouldn't be eavesdropping, Torey, she told herself. But her feet seemed to have taken root in the parquet.

A second male voice said, 'You're a first-class worrier, you know; you win all the awards.' There was a hint of laughter in the mellow baritone. 'When will you learn to seize an opportunity the instant it comes, instead of hanging about studying every angle until it's too late to do anything at all?'

'I'll admit you usually land on your feet, but——'

'And I have this time, too. I was a little concerned about being able to sell that town house of mine, you know. Housing may be in short supply in this town right now, but there isn't a lot of demand for one-bedroom town houses in that price range.'

'Watch what you're saying, Marsh—it sounds as if you think it was a mistake to buy it in the first place.'

There was no doubt about the laugh now. 'Not a mistake, exactly,' the baritone confided. 'A second bedroom in a bachelor apartment can be a serious liability.'

The other man made a sound that might have been assent. 'And now that you're getting married——'

'I'm acquiring the old family home. Perfect, wouldn't you say?'

Torey's jaw dropped. Acquiring the old family home? He said it as casually as if he were picking up a package of tacks at the hardware shop. And what did he mean, 'the old family home', anyway? It was Violet's house, and now it was hers——

'I still say you shouldn't be moving in here until the deal is firm.'

'What else was I supposed to do? I had to take the offer; my buyers wanted the town house, but they weren't willing to wait for it. And what difference does it make, anyway? If the girl makes a fuss, I'll just pay rent on the place till the sale goes through. A reasonable rent— nothing outrageous.'

A fuss, Torey thought. As if this entire invasion doesn't mean a thing to him, and shouldn't bother me in the least——

'I haven't heard a word from her, Marsh. I sent those papers more than a week ago.'

'She's probably thinking it over and talking to all her friends.'

It was funny, Torey thought, how expressive a voice could be. She knew, for instance, that he had shrugged as he'd said that.

'You're letting yourself in for all kinds of trouble, Marsh.'

'What kind of trouble can she make? And why would she want to? She's got a fast sale——'

'She can hold you up for more money.'

'She'd better not try.' The humour had faded from the baritone voice, and something very like grimness remained. 'I'm offering her a fair price for the house. Let's be honest, it's more than fair, it's downright generous. If she thinks the place is worth West Coast prices, she's wrong, and she's welcome to come back and look at it herself. But in the meantime——'

Torey stepped into the open doorway, one slim hand braced on each of the carved posts. 'Thanks,' she said crisply. 'I'm glad to have your permission, because that's exactly what I've done. I've come to look at...' she paused, and added very gently '...my house.'

The man sitting on the white leather couch looked up at her as if his worst nightmare had suddenly sprung to life in broad daylight. He grabbed for the arm of the couch and hauled himself up from the leather depths. Then, as if uncertain what to do next, he shifted his weight from one foot to the other and tugged at his unkempt blond moustache, and darted glances at Torey.

He was the worrier, she concluded, and nothing to be concerned about. She turned her attention to the other man. This was the one with the laughing baritone voice, the one who had dismissed her as unimportant, a mere trifle to be disposed of in order to get what he wanted.

He was standing with his back to the empty fireplace, one elbow propped on the carved oak mantel. His sports jacket was unbuttoned and his other hand rested easily on his hip. By the time she turned her head to look directly at him, he had concealed any surprise he might have felt at her sudden appearance. He didn't even blink.

Torey was a bit disappointed at the lack of reaction. A guilty flush might be too much to expect from someone of his calibre, she told herself, but shouldn't he at least have been startled? She put her chin up and gave him the look that some of her friends called the Farrell Searchlight—a long, direct inspection from which no personal flaw could hide.

It pained her to admit, a full minute later, that the man didn't appear to have many. He was tall and lean, with broad shoulders that tapered nicely to narrow hips. His hair was black; it looked almost too silky to be real, and for a moment she had to fight off an irrational desire to walk across the room and give it a tug, just to see if it would come off in her hands and leave him looking like a hard-boiled egg. He had a generous mouth which at the moment was pressed into a firm line. His eyes were dark, too, and fringed with lashes that were outrageously long and curly. In fact, a Roman nose was all that kept his face from being too good-looking, she decided, and concluded with a bit of spite that his flaws must be the sort that were on the inside.

His hands were big and well-shaped and looked strong enough to bend steel; a momentary whitening of his knuckles was the only sign that he might be uncomfortable under her scrutiny. It amused her a bit. So he wasn't quite so certain of himself after all, was he, this—what was it the worrier had called him? Marsh?

'Finished?' he asked drily. 'Or would you like me to turn around so you can inspect the back too?'

Torey smiled sweetly. 'Does it bother you that I want to take a good look at the person who's trying to move into my house by force?'

The removal men stopped in the hallway behind her with a large black leather reclining chair. 'Where do you want us to put this, Mr Endicott?' one of them called.

Endicott? It startled Torey, and then she remembered that he had said this was the old family home. Endicott— that would make him some relative of Violet's late husband, that was all. Well, he'd soon learn that, relative or not, this wasn't going to be his family home again.

'Put it——' he began, and then seemed to think better of it. 'Down,' he added succinctly. 'Anywhere.' His hand slipped to the back of his neck, as if it hurt.

So he isn't so dense after all, Torey thought. He knows quite well he's been caught, with no ground to stand on.

'Put it back on the van,' she contradicted crisply. 'Along with all of Mr Endicott's other possessions. Because he's not moving into my house.'

'*Your* house?' He glanced at the worrier. 'Didn't you tell the young lady——'

Torey interrupted firmly. 'I gather that you've made an offer to buy the house, Mr Endicott. Since I haven't received the offer, I couldn't say whether it's a generous one or not——'

'It's generous,' he put in.

'But it doesn't matter what it is. The house is not for sale. Thank you for your interest, gentlemen—there is the door. Oh, and if you'd give me any keys you have before you leave——'

Marsh Endicott's laugh was wonderful, a deep, rippling sound that seemed to fill the room. In other circumstances, it would have been infectious.

'I wasn't aware that I'd told some sort of joke,' Torey said stiffly. 'If you think I'm not serious about this....'

He didn't seem to hear. He was still looking at his friend. 'Don't you think you should tell the young lady the facts of life?'

Torey put her hands on her hips. 'I could call the police, you know, and have you evicted.'

'I wouldn't advise it. Stan? I think you'd better make plain to the young lady right now that she doesn't own this house.'

For an instant, Torey's head swam with the shock of it, and everything in her field of view turned slightly green. Just how had he accomplished that, anyway? A faked deed? A forged signature? Something outside the law, that was sure.

Then she started to laugh. 'That was a good try,' she said admiringly. 'But if I don't own it, why on earth are you offering to buy it from me?'

Marsh Endicott moved then, to lean indolently against the mantel with his ankles crossed, his hands deep in his trouser pockets. 'Tell her, Stan,' he invited.

For the first time since she had come into the room, Torey took a good look at the worrier. It was an appropriate name for him, she thought; it appeared at the moment as if he were about to have apoplexy. So this was Stan Spaulding, she thought. This was Violet's lawyer. From the way he had sounded on the telephone the night he had called to tell her that Violet had died and named Torey in her will, she would have thought he was a much older man.

'The offer Marsh has made is for your half of the house,' Stan Spaulding said quietly.

The words were like knives slicing through her chest. Torey was suddenly having trouble breathing. 'But——' she gasped. 'You told me—*Half* of the house?'

Stan Spaulding shuffled his feet on the worn spot on the carpet and said, 'I very foolishly told you what Violet's will said, before I checked for pre-existing conditions on the property. In actual fact, I found, Violet and her late husband owned the house as tenants in common rather than the more usual way, which is known as joint tenancy with the right of survivorship, so as a matter of practicality——'

Torey shook her head. 'I haven't the vaguest idea what you're talking about!'

Marsh Endicott cleared his throat. 'Stan, you're doing your law professor act again,' he said dispassionately.

'Miss Farrell—you *are* Victoria Farrell, aren't you? Perhaps we should ask to see identification.'

Torey wanted to stick her tongue out at him. She settled for what she hoped was a devastating glare—it would have been more effective if she hadn't had to look so far up to meet his gaze—and turned back to Stan Spaulding in the vague hope that this time his words would make sense. Considering that her head was starting to pound like a world-class earthquake, it seemed doubtful.

Marsh Endicott folded his arms across his chest and said, 'I think it might be easier if I translate, Stan. Miss Farrell, your Aunt Violet and her husband—who, by the way, had the honour of being my grandfather even before he was her husband—each owned half of this house. That's not uncommon among married couples, of course, except that they did it a little differently than most. In most cases the survivor—in this case, Violet— owns the house outright and can leave it to whomever she pleases, which in this case would be you. Or else, if the person who dies first—my grandfather—owns the house outright, he can leave the house to whomever he pleases——'

'You,' Torey said. 'Yes, I see, but——'

'—with the survivor, Violet, having the use of the house as long as she lives.'

Torey put her fingertips against her aching temples. 'This entire thing makes no sense.'

'I agree absolutely. For some unknown reason, my grandfather allowed Violet to wheedle him into giving her half of the house when they married. It was certainly not her native charm and beauty that made him do it,' he mused, 'because she was ugly as sin and would have made the average boa constrictor look like a warm and delightful pet. On the other hand——'

'Can we stick to the point?' Torey fumed.

'Of course. Sorry, I got distracted. The result is that when my grandfather died ten years ago he left his half of the house to me, with Violet having the right to use it as long as she chose. Now that Violet's dead, it's mine absolutely—there is no question of that. Meanwhile, her half, which I have to admit she had every right to dispose of as she chose...'

Torey groped for the arm of the white leather couch and sat down, hard.

'Why she did it I can only speculate,' Marsh Endicott went on airily. 'I'm sure it had something to do with the fact that on more than one occasion in the early years of her marriage my father was heard to refer to her as— well, we won't go into that. Let's just say that Violet was known for holding a grudge.'

If Marsh Endicott's father was anything like him, Torey thought, she could see Violet's point.

'I'm awfully sorry, Miss Farrell,' Stan Spaulding said miserably. 'But her will didn't say anything about the life tenancy, you see. It just said, "All real and personal property to my great-niece, Victoria Farrell," and so I assumed——'

'Careless of you, Stan,' Marsh said, but it was almost casual, as if he'd said it a great many times before. 'I told you, she was hoping the whole thing would be overlooked, or that I would be too proud to make a fight of it.'

Stan Spaulding gritted his teeth for a moment and then went on, 'As soon as I found out differently I tried to call you, Miss Farrell, but——'

'But I'd already left Los Angeles on my way here,' Torey muttered.

'And where have you been all this time?' Marsh Endicott asked curiously. 'That was nearly a week ago.'

'Not that it's any of your concern,' Torey said, 'but I'm now an expert on how much a complete brake job costs in North Platte, Nebraska, and as for fan belts, tyres, and radiator hoses...'

He raised his eyebrows at that, and then walked over to the window and tipped the ancient venetian blinds to peer out at the battered old station-wagon. What he saw must have satisfied him; he nodded and came back to the centre of the room

Stan Spaulding was saying, with determination, 'So I mailed copies of everything—both of the wills, and Marsh's offer to buy your half——'

'They'll be forwarded,' she said. 'They'll probably catch up with me in a week or two.'

'Well, there's an easier way than that,' Marsh Endicott said briskly. 'Stan had copies of everything, so we'll all just run down to his office and get the paperwork out of the way——'

'Hold it,' Torey said. 'What paperwork?'

'For the sale.'

She turned to Stan. 'Let me get this straight. Half of this house is mine without question, right?'

'Absolutely.'

'Which half?'

Stan frowned. 'Well, that's a little hard to say, actually. I mean, it's a tenancy in common, and so you each have the right to possession and use of the whole property. That means——'

'That Mr Endicott can't put a lock on the kitchen door and shut me out,' Torey said with satisfaction. 'Or make me climb a ladder to the balcony to get in and out because he's claimed the ground floor as his. Right?'

Marsh Endicott said something under his breath that Torey was glad she hadn't heard clearly. His face was beginning to resemble the sky outside—they were both dark and threatening a storm.

'That's true,' Stan said, with a judicious tug at his moustache. 'He can't.'

'Thanks a bunch, Spaulding,' Marsh Endicott muttered and turned his back on the discussion.

'But as far as the house is concerned, Miss Farrell, I really think that you should consider——'

'I have considered. I am not interested in selling my half of the house to Mr Endicott,' Torey said.

Marsh Endicott wheeled around and glared at her. 'Who the hell besides me do you think is going to buy half a house?'

'Don't you ever listen?' Torey chided. 'I told you twenty minutes ago that it's not for sale.'

'Of course it's for sale!'

'I'm going to live here.'

'You can't be serious.'

'Why can't I? It's a beautiful house.' Then, for the first time since she had burst into the big room, she took a good look at her surroundings. It was a formal parlour, unusually large for a house of the period, with elegantly carved mouldings, oak ceiling beams, and big windows, hidden just now by the dust-laden venetian blinds. The twin chandeliers could also stand a cleaning; their crystal facets were too dulled by dirt to gleam. The carpet was worn almost threadbare in spots, and the wallpaper... Torey walked over to a corner to get a better look. The wallpaper had once been livid pink. Now it was faded to the dull, blotchy shade of an overripe peach, except where Violet's pictures had obviously hung. There the pink remained, making the wall look as if it had developed an extraordinarily bad case of eczema.

'It's a wonderful house,' she added stoutly. 'It needs a little work, but it will be great when it's done. Yes, I think I'll be very happy here.'

'I suppose next you'll offer to buy my half,' Marsh snapped. 'Well, get rid of that notion. I'm damned if you're going to con me out of my share!'

'I haven't the money,' Torey said placidly. 'If I did, I'd be happy to match your generous offer—whatever it was—and then we could talk about who was trying to defraud whom.'

He growled a little, and his fists clenched.

Stan Spaulding cleared his throat and said, 'You might consider the financial realities, Miss Farrell. As you said yourself, the house needs work. And there are expenses here: real estate taxes, and high utility bills in a house this size. If you don't have any money——'

'Did I say I was destitute?' Torey asked pleasantly. 'I certainly didn't mean to. I have a perfectly good job; it's just that I don't have lumps of cash lying around. I assure you I can afford the real estate taxes, Mr Spaulding.' She smiled sweetly at Marsh Endicott. 'My half of them, at least. And I'm also willing to pay a reasonable rent...' She paused, and then deliberately and maliciously quoted him. 'Nothing outrageous, of course—to my co-owner for the use of his half of the property.'

Stan Spaulding chewed the end of his moustache. 'Still, I think it would be the wisest thing if you would just accept Marsh's offer and have the thing done with. It's really very generous, considering the appraised value of the house and everything——'

'Why should I take your word for it?' Torey asked. 'You're obviously Mr Endicott's friend.'

'He used to be,' Marsh Endicott muttered. 'I wouldn't say he's been acting too friendly today.'

'But how do I know that's a correct appraisal? Besides, you've overlooked the fact that I don't want to sell. I came out here to live, Mr Spaulding—I have all my things with me.'

'Everything you own is in that car?' Marsh Endicott walked back to the window and took another look, then shook his head. 'I doubt it will make it back to Los Angeles,' he said thoughtfully.

Torey's cynical sense of humour bubbled to the surface. 'I don't see why it wouldn't,' she murmured. 'It's half new pieces. But that's beside the point. I've just finished a five-day drive, and I'm not going off on another one.'

'All right, I'll raise my offer by the price of a first-class ticket back to Los Angeles.'

Torey gave him the sweetest, most meaningless smile in her repertoire. 'That's very generous of you. But I'm still not going anywhere. Now, since the removal men are standing here waiting for instructions, where would you like them to take your mattress? Back to your previous residence, I'd suggest.' Then she remembered that he'd sold it. Too bad, she thought. It certainly wasn't her problem...

'Upstairs.'

'But——' It was a mere squeak of protest.

His smile was just as saccharine, and just as deadly, as hers had been. 'I own half of this house, too, Miss Farrell. If you can live here, so can I. Have you got a quarter, Stan? We'll flip to see who gets the master bedroom. Unless you'd like to consider it common property—Victoria?'

CHAPTER TWO

TOREY swallowed hard and closed her eyes. I'm going to wake up, she told herself, and I'll be back in that motel in North Platte, and the brakes will be done, and I'll be ready to drive on...

Stan Spaulding said, 'Marsh, you've got to be kidding. You can't both move in here.'

'You just finished explaining the whole thing to Miss Farrell, Stan. The same rules apply to me, don't they? She can't shut me out of the house, either.'

'That's true, but——'

'Then I'm staying. As for the bedroom question, Miss Farrell——'

'I'll take heads,' Torey said grimly.

His right hand dug into his trouser pocket, and he said, under his breath, 'Well, that's certainly a relief.'

Torey glared at him. His face was almost expressionless, but there was a gleam in his eyes that she didn't trust for a moment.

He spun a coin high in the air and slapped it down on the back of his wrist. 'Heads it is,' he said. 'Congratulations, the master bedroom is yours.' He strode out to the hallway and said to the removal men, 'Bring that mattress up here. I'll find a place for it somewhere.'

It felt to Torey as if he had taken all the oxygen out of the room when he'd left; she was having a great deal of trouble breathing. She glanced at Stan Spaulding, and caught him sneaking a sideways, half-guilty look at her.

And he ought to look guilty, she thought. It was his fault she was in this mess, after all. The incompetence of the man, not to have bothered to check out the facts before telling her she'd inherited a house.

Or was it fair to put all the blame on him, when her own impetuous conduct had played such a part? If only she had waited a few days until things were truly straightened out, instead of rushing out here without even bothering to call Stan back—but it was too late for that kind of thinking. She was here, and there was no easy way to change that.

Unless, of course, she took Marsh Endicott up on his offer, and let him buy her that first-class ticket back to Los Angeles.

She straightened her shoulders with determination. Was that all the backbone she had? she asked herself. Was she such a quitter, after all, that she would run back to LA in despair, without even giving herself a chance, because things hadn't turned out quite as she expected? On the other hand, she thought drily, a man the size of Marsh Endicott was not exactly a *tiny* hitch in her plans!

'He's not always like this.' Stan's voice was a bit hesitant.

Torey said, 'You mean that sometimes he's worse?'

'Of course not. He's usually a very nice, empathetic guy.' He grinned suddenly and added, almost in a whisper, 'You're right. Sometimes he's worse. But he's not dangerous or anything. I mean, you'll be perfectly safe with him.'

Torey laughed in spite of herself.

Stan tipped his head a little to one side and watched her approvingly. 'I'm glad to see you smile,' he confided. 'I was afraid—I'm really sorry about the mix-up, you know. I should never have told you anything until I'd checked it all out. But when you asked about the will—well, it all seemed so clear, and I thought, what harm could there be in telling you?'

After that ingenuous admission, she couldn't find it in her heart to hold it against him personally. Besides, it felt as if she was going to need an ally, and Stan Spaulding looked like the best candidate she had.

'If there is anything I can do...' he said.

'I can't think of anything at the moment, but I'll keep that in mind. I'm sure I'll need some advice, getting settled in a new town and all.'

'You really meant that you're staying? You didn't just say it to annoy Marsh?'

Torey settled for the diplomatic answer. 'Yes, I meant it. I plan to stay here.'

Stan shook his head. 'Give up California for this? Why?'

'I have a project I'm working on.'

He looked puzzled, but when she didn't volunteer to go on he said, 'Well, if I can't help unload your car or anything, I'll be on my way.'

He's prudently getting out of the war zone, Torey thought. I can't say that I blame him.

She saw him out, and then remembered something she had meant to ask for, so she ran across the lawn after him. 'Mr Spaulding—those wills. I'd like to have copies of them as soon as I could.'

He nodded. 'Of course. I'll drop them off when I leave the office tonight. And call me Stan, please—I'd like it.'

She smiled and nodded and went slowly back across the lawn. She couldn't help but notice that at the house across the street the corner of a lace curtain dropped back into place as Stan drove away.

The wind had come up; she closed the front door to hold in what little heat remained in the house. Now that the warmth of that confrontation had died down, she was shivering.

The removal men hadn't come back downstairs. Torey wondered what Marsh Endicott was finding for them to

do up there, and decided that she'd better go and see
for herself. She took a deep breath and turned towards
the open stairway, half wishing that Stan hadn't been in
such a hurry to leave, half glad of the opportunity to
look around by herself.

It was easy enough to find the master bedroom. It was
directly at the head of the stairs, a big corner room right
above the parlour. The bedroom had the same wonderful, wide windows as the parlour had, with arched
panels of bevelled glass above each of them. It also had
a fireplace, smaller than the parlour one, but more elegant, surrounded with green ceramic tiles and capped
with a wonderful carved mantel. But that was all it had;
the room was completely empty. There was not a chair,
not a bed, not even a rug.

Torey stood in the doorway briefly and surveyed the
expanse of oak floor. She glanced into the adjoining
bathroom, half expecting that it would be empty, too,
but the antique fixtures were still in place. Then she followed the sound of grunts, scrapes, and occasional curses
to the back of the house, where she found the two removal men struggling to set up a king-sized bed in a
room that was almost the same dimensions as the bed
was.

Marsh Endicott moved a leather suitcase out of their
way and came to the door. His silky black eyebrows rose
a bit as he said, 'I hope it's all right with you if I use
this room. Or did you have plans for it, too?'

Torey could feel her cheeks turning pink. The first
thing she had seen was the wonderful north light in that
room, and she already mentally placed her drawing-table
at just the right angle beside the window. For a moment
she felt almost guilty; this room was going to be very
cramped for a man of his size, while she had the biggest
bedroom and no furniture at all.

'Isn't there a larger room you could use?' she asked, trying her best to be fair.

'Yes. This one, however, is right next to the back stairs, so I can tiptoe silently up and down and not disturb you——'

Torey snapped, 'Oh, do stop feeling sorry for yourself because you lost a simple coin toss! No one is forcing you to live here at all.'

'That works both ways, you know.'

She ignored that, with an effort, and said, 'I assume there used to be furniture around here. And I seem to recall that Aunt Violet's will specified that it was mine.'

'Yes,' Marsh Endicott said thoughtfully. 'There was furniture. Lovely things, too—some of them had been passed down from one generation of my ancestors to the next, right up until Violet came into the family and stole it.'

She dug her fists into her hips and stared up at him. 'If you had the nerve to steal it back...'

His grin lit up his face, she noted, as if a fire were glowing in his eyes.

'That wasn't quite what I meant to say,' she muttered.

He let it pass. 'Haven't you any more faith in Stan than that? He explained to me that it was legally yours—every chair, every table, every bit of priceless antique wood and brocade and satin——'

'Just tell me what you did with it, Endicott.'

'It's in the attic. Through the door. I had the movers haul it all up there because it was just too painful for me to look at it.'

Torey started for the attic and said, over her shoulder, 'If you expect anyone to fall for that sentimental note in your voice, you'd better practise it a little more. It's pretty thin at the moment.'

'Mr Endicott,' one of the removal men said plaintively, 'this isn't going to work. The mattress won't come in here at all.'

Marsh Endicott looked at the way the bed's framework was jammed into the room, and then turned to look speculatively at Torey. 'Do you suppose we could reconsider——?'

'No,' she said firmly. 'I won the toss, and I'm keeping the master bedroom. But if you'd like to borrow some furniture that will fit in there, I'd be happy to help you out.'

He grunted. 'For a reasonable rent, I suppose.'

Torey did her best to look innocent. 'I wouldn't dream of charging you rent. I made the offer in the spirit of co-operative living. Of course, if you'd like to have your movers carry a bed and chair down for me while they're moving your things...'

He looked around the tiny bedroom again. 'I don't suppose I have much choice,' he growled, and followed her down the short hallway to the attic door. 'Just do me a favour, Victoria.'

'I thought I already had.' The attic was dim, with dark shades drawn over the windows, and the stairs had an odd turn at the very top of the flight. She squinted, trying to let her eyes grow accustomed to the lack of light.

'Don't tell any of my friends I'm sleeping in your bed,' he begged.

She stopped, in shock, on the top step, and he ran into her. She grabbed wildly for the railing, and he reached out—almost automatically, she thought—to steady her. His hands came to rest warmly on her hip-bones. 'Don't worry,' she said breathlessly. 'I——'

He went on, ruthlessly, 'They'll all die laughing, once they got to know you, and I couldn't let that happen to my friends.'

* * *

Marsh Endicott's description of the treasures in the attic had been largely fiction; Violet's furniture was mostly too new to be antique, too old to be stylish, and too nearly worn out to be comfortable. But Torey found a rather wonderful four-poster bed in the furthest and most dusty corner, and enough odds and ends to make the master bedroom look inviting.

A couple of hours later she dusted off her hands and looked around her room with satisfaction. Her drawing-table was assembled and stood in a corner where the best light would fall over her left shoulder. The worst of the faded spots on the wallpaper were covered by framed prints she had found in a hall cupboard. The brass light fixtures gleamed from the vigorous polishing they had received. There was a crushed-velvet chair beside the fireplace, at the corner of a faded old Persian rug. There was a small table beside the bed with a decent reading lamp and a new book waiting on it, to help her feel at home as she settled in for the night.

'A light dinner, a hot bath, and an early bedtime,' she prescribed for herself. 'And tomorrow, you start to work.'

For an instant, a familiar wobbly feeling gripped her stomach. It was raw fear, and Torey had no trouble diagnosing it. What if this didn't work? What if she couldn't produce what she had promised?

She stood beside the drawing-table, where a blank sheet of her favourite smooth-surfaced paper was already taped down and ready, and saw in her mind's eye a neat, rectangular panel. It was hauntingly, mockingly empty, waiting for life and humour to be infused. But could she do that?

'Of course I can,' she said firmly. 'I've been drawing cartoons all my life. This is just——'

Different, she thought with a sort of unpleasant thud. Because it was no amusing little hobby now. This was the big time, and the days were slipping away...

She forced herself to breathe slowly and will the fear away. It was becoming harder, she admitted, each time she had to do it.

There hadn't been time for a trip to the supermarket. She'd have to do that tomorrow, she decided, as she looked at the contents of Violet's kitchen cabinets. All she could find was staple fare in cans and boxes, and most of it was unexciting. She opened a can of clam soup and put it on the old-fashioned range to heat while she looked for crackers.

Still, she thought, as boring as the contents of the cabinets were, it was better than looking at the outside of them. Whatever had inspired Violet Endicott to paint her entire kitchen lime-green? And, having done so, where had she got the inspiration to stencil smudgy pink and yellow flowers on every cabinet door and along every straight line in the entire room?

Marsh came in the back door as she was eating a second bowl of soup, and Torey sighed inwardly. He had left right after the removal van had departed, and there had been a faint hope in her heart, she supposed, that he might not come back at all.

He paused on the threshold with the door held open, as if he was surprised to see her there. Torey felt the blast of cold air; she forced herself not to look up from her book. 'It's only now warming up after your movers let all the heat out,' she said politely. 'And while the size of the heating bill may not be a matter of concern for you, it certainly is for me. Would you close the door?'

He did. 'Do you plan to do this regularly?'

'Do you mean sitting at the kitchen table reading? It is my kitchen—half of it, anyway. Or are you implying that I'm nagging you about the door?'

'Actually, I was referring to the raid on my pantry supplies.' He picked up the empty clam soup can.

Her eyes widened. 'Oh, rot. I never thought—I assumed that Aunt Violet would have a few things left when...' She stumbled to a halt. When was she going to learn to stop assuming things?

'She did, but who knows how long they'd been here? Never mind, Victoria. What's a can of clam chowder between friends?' The question was dry.

'We're not friends, and we're not likely to be. I'll replace the soup tomorrow,' she said stiffly. She pushed her dish away; the clam soup didn't taste as good all of a sudden. 'We'll just have to work out a schedule for using the kitchen, I suppose, or we'll be tripping over each other all the time.'

He looked at her for a long moment. Then he pulled a folded manilla envelope out of his pocket and tossed it on the table. 'Stan Spaulding sent those things over for you.'

She slid a finger under the flap and pulled out a sheaf of papers. 'Thanks for doing me the favour of delivering them.'

'Don't choke on the gracious phrase—you know quite well I didn't do it as a favour. The offer I made to buy your half is in there, too.'

He draped his down-filled jacket over the back of a chair and put a kettle of water on to heat. When he came back to the table, he pulled a chair around so he could straddle it with his arms folded across the back.

As if it's a fence to protect him from me, Torey thought.

He had exchanged the sports jacket for more casual clothes. Still, this was obviously a gentleman of means, she thought; that sweater hadn't come off any ordinary rack. It was obviously hand-knitted, and the bold grey and black pattern emphasised the breadth of his shoulders.

'Aren't you even going to look at it, Victoria?' he asked.

Torey shrugged and turned the papers over. 'By the way, no one has called me Victoria since I was three and learned how to throw a tantrum,' she said. 'I answer much better to Torey. Is Marsh short for something else?' She looked up at him ingenuously. 'If we are going to be living under the same roof, I thought——'

'Are we? I was hoping that would change your mind.' He gestured at the paper in her hand.

His full name, she noted from the legal documents, was David Marshall Endicott. She filed that knowledge away—it might come in handy some time—and skimmed the papers, ignoring the legal language and looking only for the all-important figures.

Then she shrugged. 'It might be a very generous offer for Springhill, but——'

'Yes, it is. A couple of years ago you'd have been lucky to get half of that, but some of our industries have expanded, and there's a housing shortage here right now. So before you say anything else about appraisals——'

'I wasn't planning to,' Torey murmured.

'Just remember that this isn't California. Housing shortage or not, real estate simply isn't worth the amount of money here that it is on the West Coast.'

'I know. That's mainly why I'm here.'

He shook his head a little as if to clear it.

'The cost of living is cheaper,' Torey said patiently.

'I don't understand.' He jerked a thumb at the paper she was holding. 'If you've got the sort of job that allows you to turn up your nose at that kind of money, why in hell are you worried about the high cost of living? And, speaking of jobs, what sort of job allows you to flit off across the country to live? You did say you have a job, didn't you?'

'I'm a freelance commercial artist,' Torey said crisply. 'I can draw just as well in Springhill as in Los Angeles. My clients seldom see me anyway, so there's no reason why I can't use the telephone and the mail to keep in touch.' It was all true; the fact that it wasn't quite the entire truth certainly wasn't any of his business. 'And— as I said—it costs me less to live here, especially now that I don't have to pay rent. Do you know what it costs for an apartment in LA these days?'

He looked at her for a long while and then said, 'I think I need a cup of coffee.'

Torey felt the same way, but she would have bitten off her tongue before begging for one. He came back to the table with two cups of black, steaming instant coffee, however, and pushed one across to her as if daring her to refuse it.

'Victoria,' he began, confidingly. 'Sorry—Torey. You don't understand the problem I've got at the moment. I'm getting married in six months——'

'I know. I can hardly wait to meet her,' Torey said gravely.

'Why? So you can create trouble? Don't count on being able to do it.'

'I wouldn't dream of trying. I just wanted to see the kind of woman who would find you attractive, that's all.'

He didn't take the bait, but she thought he had to restrain himself a bit. 'Kimberley and I understand each other very well,' he said instead. 'But the point is, I'm sure you can see that it's going to take most of that six months to get all the necessary work done to this house. Take this mess, for example.' He waved an all-encompassing hand at the room.

'Do you mean she isn't a fan of lime-green kitchens?' Torey counted it off on her fingers. 'Six months—that means a September wedding. Didn't she want to be a June bride?'

He sighed. 'I can't see what business it is of yours, but summer is her busiest season. She's a travel agent.'

'Oh? That should make for an interesting honey-moon——'

'You are trying to avoid the point, Victoria! This entire thing is impossible. For example, how can I remodel a master bedroom if you're living in it?'

'That could be a problem,' Torey said agreeably. 'But it was your idea to flip a coin for it.'

'It was an idiotic thing to suggest, but I suppose I was in shock. I went to Stan's office tonight to talk about the alternatives. He says that if you won't sell me your half——'

'I'm still not excited by the idea, no.'

'Then my only alternative is to file what's called a partition action. It asks the court to order the sale of the house, with the proceeds split between us.'

Torey frowned. She reached for her pencil and doodled on the paper napkin. 'What will that accomplish? Then neither of us will have the house.'

'It would probably be auctioned.'

'And you'll be at the auction with bags full of cash. I see.' The doodle was taking shape as a tall, dark man in a cloak bending over a tiny blonde who was securely tied to a railroad track.

What a cliché, Torey told herself. You can do a whole lot better than that, Farrell. She crumpled the napkin.

'So why are you telling me all this?' she asked. 'Shouldn't you be keeping it a deep, dark secret until you can spring the legal papers on me?'

'Because the partition action will take time, and it will be expensive. I want to have the matter over with so I can get to work. Besides, I am not made of money, and I'd much rather pay carpenters than lawyers.'

'What do you do? I'm curious——'

'I'm going to end up with this house, Torey, whatever it takes. It's only right that I have it; it's my family home, not yours. Violet should never have had her hands on it at all.'

'Too bad for you that your grandfather didn't agree.'

He ignored the interruption. 'But I'd rather do it neatly, and fast. So I'm increasing that offer by five thousand dollars, if you'll sign it within twenty-four hours.' He leaned across the table and tapped a long finger on the paper in question.

'And you say you're not made of money,' Torey chided. 'I think I'll hold out for a while and see just how high you'll go.' She gathered up her dishes and carried them over to the sink. He did not respond, and she turned around after a couple of minutes, a little uneasy about the silence. What she saw did not reassure her.

He had put his chin down on his wrists, which were crossed on the back of the chair, and he was studying her, his dark eyes wandering slowly from her short, elfin-styled blonde hair to her stocking-clad feet and missing nothing along the way. She was perversely glad that she had changed her clothes before starting to clean her bedroom; her running-suit was the most comfortable outfit she owned, but that was the kindest thing that could be said about it. It was faded and baggy and scruffy, and, if she had been purposely trying to conceal any feminine charm, it would have been the perfect choice.

No, it was certainly not a costume to pique the interest of any young man. So why was he staring at her as if she had just walked off an alien spaceship?

She didn't realise that she had been nervously shifting her weight from one foot to the other, twisting her toes inside the bright Argyle socks, until Marsh grinned and said, 'Fair is fair, don't you think? You had your chance to look me over this afternoon. You're in no danger from me, you know, if that's what you're worried about.'

'It hadn't occurred to me,' Torey said crisply. 'I hadn't forgotten about . . . whatever-her-name-is.'

He frowned. 'Kimberley.'

'Ah, yes. I won't forget it again. I'm looking forward to meeting her. Perhaps we'll be the best of friends, and together she and I can learn to cook and keep house and——'

His face darkened a bit. 'That would certainly be cosy.'

'Wouldn't it, though?' Torey feigned a yawn. 'I'll do my best to stay out of your way, Marsh. Just for my own information, however, and not because I'm a prude or anything, am I likely to run into Kimberley in the hallways in the wee hours of the morning?'

'Not likely.'

'Does that mean she's a heavy sleeper, or aren't you expecting her to stay the night?'

'She's in Paris at the moment, conducting a three-week tour of Europe for a group of senior citizens.'

'Oh. No wonder you're exhibiting such relaxed grace and such a calm view of the world,' Torey said sweetly. 'Sleep well, Marsh. And pleasant dreams.'

She said it with a perfectly straight face, remembering the narrow, brass-railed bed that the removal men had brought down for him. He was obviously thinking about it, too; as she left the room he propped his elbows on the chair back and put his face down into his hands.

By the time she had reached her own room, however, the perfect exit line had lost much of its punch. She stared at the blank paper on the drawing-table and then tossed herself down in the velvet chair by the fireplace and for the first time let herself really think about what she had got into. Violet's house wasn't the simple and inexpensive cottage she had expected. The heating bill alone... She shivered a little at the thought.

Was she a complete fool to have turned down the money Marsh had offered? He had been right about one thing: it would support her for months. It would give her the freedom she needed to work.

For a while, she told herself. But in a matter of months, the money would be gone, spent on necessities, and if she hadn't succeeded in her quest she would have to return to the regular working world and say goodbye to her dream. She would have to go back to snatching odd moments at her drawing-board for her real work, because the rest of her days would again be occupied in feeding and clothing herself.

On the other hand, if she held on to Violet's house, she would always have it. Perhaps it wasn't going to be as easy as she had hoped, but she could still live less expensively here than in LA. With her dreams to nourish her, she could hold out for as long as she needed to, until she was a success. And once the money started to come...

Besides, she thought, just turning Violet's house over to Marsh without a fuss didn't seem right. If Violet had wanted him to have it, she could have arranged it easily enough. But Violet had been stubbornly determined to see that he wouldn't get it at all. And Torey had inherited a considerable portion of Aunt Violet's obstinacy.

'I'm going to end up with this house,' he had said. It hadn't sounded like a threat, more like a simple statement of fact. And his very assurance had made Torey more determined that he wasn't going to get his way so easily.

If he hadn't tried to force the issue, she thought, she might have felt differently. If he hadn't simply assumed that he was entitled to the house, she might have felt a bit of sympathy for his cause. But the fact was, he had moved in without so much as asking whether she wanted to sell, without concerning himself about her feelings or her right to claim this house. And she certainly needed it more than he did. So Marsh Endicott could just live with the consequences of his rash move. She had a sneaking hunch that it might be the first time anyone had ever told that young man 'no'.

Well, she'd simply stay out of his way. The house was big enough for both of them, and she would just pretend that this was an apartment complex and Marsh was a particularly annoying neighbour. She would certainly have plenty to keep her busy, without leaving a moment to think about him.

The yawn was a real one this time. She cast a wishful glance at the fireplace; it would be nice to have a crackling blaze, if only it weren't so blasted much work to haul the wood up the stairs. No, tonight she'd just have her bath and curl up with her book.

She draped the running-suit over the high footboard of the bed, wrapped herself in a pink terrycloth robe, and went into the adjoining bathroom. It must have been the only one when the house had been built, and the deep, claw-footed bath was an original. Tonight, the thought of steaming water and bubbles all the way to her chin was a very inviting one.

Thank heaven, she thought, that there was a second bath. She'd spotted it this afternoon, tucked away between Marsh's room and the attic stairway, and wondered fleetingly why Aunt Violet had spent money on such a luxury. 'Don't look a gift horse in the mouth,' she ordered herself. 'And thank heaven that you don't have to cope with sharing a bathroom with the man. He's guaranteed to be the impossible sort who leaves hair in the sink. I wonder if Kimberley has figured that out yet.'

She dropped the plug into the drain and twisted the old-fashioned tap wide open, and watched in horror as steaming water began to foam up in the bath—water so rusty that it was almost the colour of tomato juice.

Then, as she stared, too shaken even to reach for the handle, the steam of water stopped pouring into the bath and began spraying horizontally across the room from the base of the tap instead.

CHAPTER THREE

TOREY was already calling Marsh's name when she reached the bottom of the stairs. She turned towards the kitchen, panic making her bare feet slip on the polished floors. 'Marsh? The faucet's gone crazy and I don't know what to do——'

She pulled up short in the kitchen doorway. Across the room, sitting at the table with a cup of coffee between her hands, was one the prettiest redheads Torey had ever seen. For a moment the only thing Torey could think of was, She looks familiar.

The woman raised her cup to her lips, and on her left hand a huge solitaire diamond flashed fire.

'Damn,' Torey said, under her breath. A split second later, she thought, But this can't be Kimberley; he said she's in Paris. So what kind of a harem does he have? And here I stand looking like a floozie!

For an instant she could almost step outside her body and take a good look at the picture she must present, hovering there in the doorway, her hair ruffled, her long legs bare to an almost indecent height, cleansing cream smeared on her face...

That's some comfort, she thought. No woman in her right mind could think I'd deliberately come downstairs looking like this.

Marsh hadn't even looked up. 'It's your bathroom,' he pointed out succinctly.

'All right,' Torey said. 'If you can't take care of it, call a plumber. I would, but I'm afraid I don't know any. I warn you, however, that in about a minute there's going to be water pouring through the dining-room ceiling. Does that concern you, or does all that lovely sculptured plaster belong to me too?'

He pushed his chair back with a screech and stalked out of the room without a word.

The redhead laughed. 'Did you do that deliberately? Challenge his manhood by implying that he couldn't fix a little leak in the plumbing?'

Torey tightened the belt on her robe. 'I wouldn't exactly call it a little leak,' she began cautiously.

'Congratulations. I haven't seen Marsh Endicott so neatly handled in years.' The redhead set her cup down and held out a hand. 'I'm Stephanie Kendall—your neighbour back across the ravine. We met this afternoon, actually, when you asked me for directions.'

'Of course. I knew I'd seen you somewhere.' The pieces snapped into place in Torey's mind. Of course this wasn't Kimberley; there was a narrow gold wedding band just below the stunning diamond. She hadn't quite recognised the woman because this afternoon that glorious auburn hair had been hidden by the hood of a raincoat. And now, she thought, she's come over to find out what's really going on in Violet Endicott's house. You'd better get used to it, Torey—this isn't likely to be the last caller who pops in to pry!

Don't be unkind, she told herself. It's only normal for people to be curious. The neighbours, Marsh's friends... Suddenly she felt very lonely.

'I brought you a house-warming gift,' Stephanie said. 'Just a casserole—Marsh already put it in the refrigerator. I thought it would come in handy while you're getting settled.'

'That's very thoughtful.'

'Marsh implied that you might be staying for a while to get Violet's affairs straightened out.'

There was not a hint of the raging curiosity the woman must be feeling, Torey thought. There was, in fact, nothing but pleasantness in that warm voice, and she couldn't help but respond to it. She wondered if Marsh had, too, or if he was simply trying to side-track the inevitable gossip by announcing his version of the facts.

'Yes, I'm staying—for more than just a while, too, and it's got nothing to do with Violet's affairs.' There was no answer from the redhead, but her eyebrows arched ever so slightly. Torey went on, 'And it's not because I fell in love with Marsh's charm at first sight, either.'

'Believe me, no one knows Marsh would dream of thinking that!' The tone was straightforward, but there was a twinkle in Stephanie's eyes.

Torey leaned across the table confidingly. 'What does he do?' she asked. 'The only thing I can think of that he'd be ideal for is a career in organised crime.' She reached for a scrap of paper and with a few lines created a caricature: Marsh in dark sunglasses and a double-breasted raincoat with the collar turned up about his face, and an exaggerated bump under his arm where a shoulder holster would rest. 'The management end, of course,' she went on, tossing the sketch across the table. 'I can't quite see him taking orders from anyone.'

Stephanie laughed. 'Well, you're right about management. He runs the family business; it's a wholesale supply house for electrical and plumbing parts——'

Torey choked on a giggle that would not be restrained.

'You honestly didn't know that? No, obviously you didn't.' Stephanie held the sketch up to the light. 'You're quite talented. You're a commercial artist, Marsh said.'

Torey nodded.

'What sort of thing do you draw?'

'Fashion sketches for advertising layouts, mostly, but whatever the client needs—logos for businesses, designs for stationery, all sorts of things. Pretty boring, actually.' Then something—loneliness, perhaps, or the feeling of isolation in a new town, or the soothing effect of Stephanie Kendall's friendliness—cracked the tight reserve inside her mind. 'But really I'm a cartoonist,' she said, very softly. 'I've always drawn political stuff, one-shot gags, that sort of thing. But now... one of the syndicates really likes my stuff, and if I can just pull my ideas for a comic strip together in the next couple of months...' Her voice trailed off; she was half shocked at herself for saying it aloud, to a woman she'd only just met.

'So you've come out to where life is quiet to try?' Stephanie looked again at the sketch of Marsh and smiled. 'Let me know if you need anything—I'll do what I can to help,' she said. She pushed her chair back and reached for her coat. 'I have to go home; my husband will be putting the kids to bed already. Follow the path across the ravine and come visit me any time you like. It's a nice little walk and perfectly safe, even at midnight.'

'That's very kind. Are you at home all the time?'

Stephanie smiled wryly. 'Officially, I'm supposed to be taking a few months off with a new baby, and trying to decide if I want to go back to work at all. In practical fact it means I only work about three days a week instead of all the time.'

'What do you do?'

There was a note of hesitation—almost of reluctance—in Stephanie's voice. 'I sell houses.'

As soon as she was gone, Torey scrambled through the papers on the kitchen table. She hadn't been looking at the details earlier, and besides, only Marsh's name had meant anything to her.

Sure enough, there it was. Stephanie Kendall was the estate agent who had arranged the entire thing.

Torey sat down at the table. She wanted to cry, but
she told herself grimly that it would certainly do no good.
It was too late to take back what she had told Stephanie,
and that meant Marsh would soon know it too; Stephanie
was his friend, after all, not Torey's, despite the rapport
they had seemed to share. Of course she would do anything she could to help him buy the house, and not only
because it would make Marsh happy—Stephanie would
get no commission unless there was a sale.

You've just given him all the information he needs to
sabotage you, Farrell, Torey told herself. Do you have
a powerful self-destructive instinct, or what? Why don't
you just go and commit suicide...

She gathered the papers up and carried them upstairs
with her. She felt cold all of a sudden—deadly cold.

The bathroom door was open, and Marsh was sitting
on the high, curved edge of the bath with a wrench in
his hand. Blessedly, the spray had stopped; the tap
handles were lying on the white tiles at his feet, and he
was tinkering with the insides of the mechanism and
whistling softly, tunelessly, through his teeth. It was not
a contented sound, and it stopped when she appeared in
the doorway.

'Did you and Stephanie have a nice chat?' he asked
coolly.

'As a matter of fact, yes.'

'Well, don't count on the gossip flying. She's the most
discreet woman I know.'

Torey considered that, and dismissed it. Discretion was
one thing and secrecy another. Stephanie might not
spread what she knew, but she'd certainly tell Marsh.

'I didn't realise you had company when I came flying
down the stairs,' she offered, 'or I'd have been a bit
more discreet myself. Perhaps we should rig up a warning
bell or something—it would save a lot of embarrassment.'

'Why bother?' he asked coolly. 'You don't seem to embarrass easily. I see you're still running around half-naked.'

Abruptly, Torey was no longer cold; in fact, she was boiling with fury. The man was completely unreasonable. With the bathroom door standing open, he'd have had a ringside seat if she had got dressed. And—judging from what she already knew about Marsh—he'd probably have been even more upset if she had!

He didn't seem to notice her irritation. 'The faucet is no big problem.'

Torey forced herself to speak calmly. 'That's a relief. I didn't break it on purpose, you know, just so I could come running downstairs and make a scene.'

He grunted a little, as if he didn't believe her. 'Some new washers and a good lubricant and it will hold together for a while longer.'

That didn't sound terribly promising to Torey, but she bit her tongue; what did she know about plumbing, after all?

'But from there on...' He shook his head.

She perched on the opposite side of the bath. 'The rust, you mean?'

'Rusty water means old pipes and bad connections. I had already assumed that every pipe in the whole house should be replaced, but I hadn't expected it to be quite this bad. The damned bathtub hasn't been used in years.'

Torey wrinkled her nose. 'Surely that can't be. Aunt Violet must have taken a bath now and then.'

He shot a look at her. 'I thought witches tried never to get wet—sorry. She was an invalid for the last couple of years. She probably had her baths in bed, and her live-in nurse used the other bathroom.'

'Oh, that explains why it's there.'

'That's why.' He set the tap handles neatly on the edge of the old-fashioned pedestal sink. 'At least it isn't spraying any more. I'll give you the name of a good plumber.' He handed her the wrench, and said, in an absolutely level voice that did not quite mask the fiendish twinkle in his eyes, 'Unless the pride of ownership makes you feel that you'd rather do it yourself? I could loan you a book of instructions, if you'd like.'

He was quiet in the morning, she had to grant him that; she hadn't heard a single sound, but by the time she roused from a restless sleep he was already gone. Her cautious survey of the house, in a much more concealing robe than the short terry one she'd been wearing the night before, found few signs of his presence. There was a coffee-cup and spoon on the kitchen counter, right next to the telephone directory—it was open to the listings for plumbers, and a name was circled in heavy black ink. That was all the evidence she found that Marsh had even been there that morning.

And he hadn't left hair in the bathroom sink, either. Torey was vaguely disappointed, but not as much as she was a moment later when she discovered that Violet's nurse had never installed a lock on her bathroom door.

'Of course not,' she told herself wryly. 'Who was going to walk in on her? Not Violet, that's sure.'

She took a very fast shower, just in case some imp of fate suggested to Marsh that he come back to the house; it seemed only prudent to anticipate that sort of thing. Then she called the plumber and settled down at her drawing-table, one ear tuned for the doorbell.

It rang more times than she could count: first a door-to-door opinion pollster, then a perfume salesman, then a gospel preacher. If she hadn't known better, Torey thought, she would have suspected them all of being curious neighbours in disguise. After the plumber finally turned up, she stopped answering the bell, but she couldn't ignore it altogether—it sounded like an entire church carillon, and it chimed for almost as long.

Between each interruption she returned to the drawing-table. By late afternoon the waste-paper basket at her feet overflowed with crumpled pages, and her hand ached, not from drawing but from clutching her pencil too tightly in frustration. Finally she admitted that she was getting nowhere—the only good piece of art she had executed all day was on the beige wallpaper right next to her drawing-board, where she had absent-mindedly turned a big brown water-spot into a caricature of Marsh. So she laid out a fresh sheet of paper and sharpened her pencils and turned the lights off with a firm snap.

Tomorrow, she promised herself. It will be different tomorrow.

The kitchen was smelling heavenly, and two place-settings of Violet's hand-painted china were already laid at the round oak table, when she heard Marsh's key in the lock. He paused just inside the back door. 'Sorry if you're expecting company, but I wasn't planning to go out tonight.'

Torey turned from the oven, her cheeks flushed a little from the heat, but mostly from having to face him. 'Good,' she said. 'Because I wasn't expecting company— just you.'

His eyebrows raised so far that she thought for a moment they might stick permanently in that position. 'Now that's a surprise,' he said gently. 'You didn't strike me as the sort who'd like to... play house.'

She bristled at the smooth implication. 'Well, don't take it as an invitation, because it's not. It's only the casserole Stephanie brought last night—it's big enough for two.'

He sniffed the air. 'Are you certain of that? Stephanie knows perfectly well that her Hungarian chicken is my all-time favourite food.'

'There will be plenty for you. After my encounter with the plumber this afternoon, I have very little appetite.' She spooned the savoury casserole on to the plates and got two crisp green salads from the refrigerator.

'He actually showed up today?' Marsh was washing his hands at the kitchen sink; he didn't turn around. 'The whole town must be talking about you already— if his curiosity wasn't piqued, he'd have been too busy to come till next week.'

Torey bit her tongue and spread her napkin out carefully across her lap. You don't attack a man right before you ask him for a favour, she reminded herself. 'He gave me an estimate on the work. I can't afford it, Marsh.'

It didn't seem to bother him. 'That's one of the crosses that home-owners have to bear, Torey.' He stirred his chicken with his fork and inhaled its spicy fragrance with appreciation. 'How did you plan to take care of the necessary work when you thought you'd inherited the whole thing?'

'Is it a crime that I never gave a thought to the plumbing?' Torey asked crossly. 'It sounds to me as though they're making water pipes out of solid gold these days! In any case, I thought Aunt Violet probably lived in a sensible, snug little bungalow—— '

'With vines creeping up the walls, under the clapboards, and between the bricks of the chimney.'

'You sound gloomy.'

'No, just realistic. In any case, I made a promise, and I'll keep it. It hasn't been twenty-four hours yet, so you can have your extra five thousand dollars when you sign that sales contract.'

'Wait a minute. I just meant——' She swallowed hard; pride was a difficult thing to choke down. 'You said last night that all the plumbing needs to be replaced. Obviously you were already planning to do that when you moved in. I just thought that, if you'll go ahead and do the bathroom, I'll pay you back my half as soon as I can.'

The silence dragged out, while her words seemed to echo in her head. It sounded idiotic even to her own ears. Why would he even consider doing her such a favour, anyway?

'Who said I was going to volunteer to pay half?' He sounded only mildly interested.

'I know, it's my bathroom,' Torey snapped. 'Well, I certainly can't afford to pay the whole bill.'

'Do you want to sell?' he asked patiently.

'No!'

'Then I don't do the plumbing. And I'm not a banker, either—if you want a loan, I'd suggest First National.'

'You've got this all figured out, haven't you? Perhaps what I should really look for is a neutral plumber and get a second opinion.' She stared across at him. 'You fixed the bid, didn't you?' she whispered. 'You arranged for it to be so expensive!'

'I wish I had,' Marsh muttered. 'But I didn't happen to think of it. No, Torey, that's what it would cost me, too.'

Not even the most accomplished liar could have sounded so sincere. With her last hope dead, Torey stared at her plate, wishing she could just sink through the floor. 'Then I'm going to have to keep using your bathroom till I save up enough money to fix mine, you know.' But it was an empty threat; she couldn't really see that bothering him—at least, not as much as it bothered her.

'Please don't leave toothpaste in the sink,' he suggested politely, and dug into his Hungarian chicken as if he didn't have a care in the world.

That left her with nothing more to say, and so it was almost a relief for Torey when the banging started at the back door. It was impossible to ignore it; there was a glass panel in the door, so whoever stood there could see quite clearly that they were in the kitchen.

'Damn,' Marsh muttered. 'I never had this trouble at the town house. No one ever knew when I was home.'

'Too bad you didn't stay there!'

He didn't answer; he just looked longingly at his half-empty plate and then went to answer the door.

A tiny old lady stood there, clutching a glass cake plate and an ebony walking-stick. Torey wondered how she had found the strength to make that ferocious noise; the lady looked scarcely strong enough to stand up. On the plate perched a tall chocolate cake. As Torey watched, the lady's hands trembled, the cake plate tipped, and the top layer slid precariously towards the edge. With great presence of mind, Marsh caught the whole thing just moments before it would have skidded on to the floor.

The lady heaved a gigantic sigh, as if she was very pleased to have her burden off her hands, and announced, 'I won't come in. I just wanted to tell you how pleasant it is to see young people moving into the neighbourhood—just like it was years ago when my husband and I moved in. He's gone now, of course. I'm Agnes Moore, and I live just across the street. And you are…?' She looked enquiringly up at Marsh.

'Marsh Endicott,' he said obediently. He was looking at the cake, which he was still holding; Torey could almost see his nose twitching.

'Endicott?' Mrs Moore repeated. 'Are you a relative of Violet's, then, Mr Endicott?'

'Only by marriage,' Marsh said gravely. 'Victoria is Violet's niece.' He gestured towards Torey.

'Well, how nice for you.' She said sweetly. 'I won't stay and interrupt your supper. And don't you worry a bit about sending me a thank-you note for the cake. It's just a little thing—I'm so glad whenever a young family moves in.'

The ebony walking-stick had tapped across the back porch and along the pavement that ran around the corner of the house before Torey found her voice.

'A young family? You realise what she thinks, don't you?' she announced. 'And you walked right into it. You could have specified that it wasn't a marriage between *us* that you were referring to!'

Marsh was sniffing the cake. 'This is fudge frosting,' he said happily. 'Real fudge frosting.'

'I know—it's your second-favourite food!'

'Nobody ever brought this kind of thing to the town house.'

'Honestly, Marsh, would you stop drooling over that cake? Don't you have any sense at all? You practically told her——'

He set the cake down reluctantly, right beside his plate. 'Do you think the old dear would have been happier if I'd told the truth? Then she'd have thought we're living here in sin.'

'She probably would have been thrilled—every time I answered the door today she was watching from her front window!'

'She was probably thinking about when to deliver the cake.'

'Well, you're the one who will have to explain it to your fiancée. I'm certainly not going to get involved!'

'I doubt Mrs Moore frequents the travel agency. And as for my explaining things to Kimberley—are we going to be doing anything that will need explaining?' It was calm, with only a vague hint of interest.

She was speechless.

'Close your mouth, Victoria,' he advised. 'It isn't at all attractive hanging open that way. Don't fret about it. Kimberley isn't seventy and half blind.'

'That's exactly my point——' She stopped dead. It had been such a smoothly phrased insult that for a moment she hadn't even recognised it. Kimberley won't

need two looks at you to know that you aren't any threat
to her—that was what he had really said.

'Oh, never mind,' she said crossly. She stirred her casserole. Any appetite she might have had was gone.
'Marsh, about the plumbing...'

He sighed. 'I thought we had settled the question of
the plumbing. I am not——'

'Aren't you any sort of gambler?' Torey challenged.
'Aren't you willing to bet on yourself? You told me last
night that you were going to end up with this house.
Well, just how certain are you that you'll own it some
day?'

He frowned a little, as if he was turning it over and
over in his mind. 'Very certain, as a matter of fact.
But——'

'Well, I'm offering you a chance to get a head start
on the work that you're going to end up doing anyway.'

His eyes narrowed.

She gave him her most charming smile, and added,
blandly, 'If, that is, I decide to sell, in the end.'

'You will. I'll give you six weeks, tops, to get tired of
the charm of rural America and start longing for the
bustle of the city. If people like Mrs Moore are already
annoying you....'

Torey shrugged. 'Perhaps you're right. So why
shouldn't you have six weeks' worth of work done by
then?'

He didn't answer.

'Aren't you scared that I might not be quite so pre-
dictable after all?' she challenged. 'Obviously a lot of
people are very happy in this town. You might be wrong
about me, Marsh.'

The silence stretched out for a long time while he stared
at one of the smudgy flowers that bordered the ceiling.

Torey smiled a little, inside, and took a bite of
Hungarian chicken. He was right, she decided; even
lukewarm, it was delectable.

'You know,' he said thoughtfully, 'I talked to Stephanie today.'

Torey's heart jolted into her throat, and the chicken felt like a rock in her stomach.

'She told me you're under a lot of pressure, trying to put together a new project.'

Well, it was no worse than I expected, Torey thought stoutly. It was inevitable that she would tell him.

'And she told me that if I wanted you to leave,' Marsh murmured, 'I'd better give you all the encouragement I can. Make your working conditions as peaceful and calm as possible. Not interfere with your concentration... she had a whole list of helpful suggestions.' He pushed his chair back and crossed the kitchen to get a clean plate and a large knife.

'You're kidding.' It was only a cracked whisper, and Torey cleared her throat and said, a little louder, 'She did?'

'Because if you're successful, she said, you could live anywhere you choose.'

She started to breathe again. Yes, it was possible that Stephanie had misunderstood her intentions. Torey hadn't really said that she intended to stay. I'll do what I can to help, Stephanie had said. Well, Torey wasn't about to turn down a gift like this!

'And that would certainly not be Springhill, would it?' He cut an enormous wedge from the chocolate cake.

'If I could live anywhere at all?' She considered it and said, 'Probably not.' It wasn't a lie, after all; if money were not a consideration, she'd probably end up on the Riviera.

He smiled a little. 'That's what I thought. The bustle of the city is already beginning to sound alluring, isn't it? What the heck, the bathroom is worth the gamble. But there are limits.'

'Like what?' Torey asked warily.

'I'll only do it if you'll swap bedrooms. If I'm going to invest in that bath, I want to keep a close eye on the work, and enjoy it when it's done.'

She almost refused without even an instant's consideration. Give up that lovely big room, after all the work she'd gone to just last night to get settled in it?

But what was she giving up, after all? It was only pure chance that she'd won the toss for the master bedroom in the first place, and it certainly hadn't turned out to be any big stroke of luck for her. If that coin had turned up tails, they wouldn't be having this argument, and the plumber could have started work this afternoon...

Marsh's room might be tiny, but it actually had better light for her work. And if she gave in gracefully she'd soon have a private bathroom again. If she stood firm, it would be a long time before she could afford to have the work done.

I'm getting out of the whole thing pretty cheaply, really, she thought. Marsh was obviously eager to swap. She didn't blame him; after one night in that narrow brass bed, he must be desperate to get his own set up again...

'I just cleaned that bedroom from floor to ceiling.'

'Very thoughtful of you.' He polished off the last few crumbs and looked at the rest of the cake.

'I suppose you've already sabotaged the other bathroom,' she said grimly.

'Nope. And I won't—I wouldn't do anything to interfere with your concentration.'

'Is that a faithful promise, not just a convenient one?'

He crossed his heart. 'Boy Scouts' honour.'

'I'll bet you were thrown out of the troop,' Torey grumbled. 'All right, I'll deal. Let's go move my drawing-board. Or are you going to insist on consuming that entire cake first?'

CHAPTER FOUR

THEY had to wait a full week for the plumber to come.

'See?' Marsh told Torey the night he telephoned the man for the third time. 'I told you he was only curious about you, or he wouldn't have shown up at all that day you called him.'

'Maybe,' Torey retorted, 'the problem is that he doesn't like to work for you. If you had only let me handle it——'

'All except for the money, you mean,' Marsh murmured.

Torey retreated into offended silence, and Marsh rewarded her with his most charming smile and reached for the telephone as it rang again. His eyebrows shot up, and he handed it to Torey with a pseudo-tactful whisper. 'It's a male.'

'I do know a few,' she snapped. It turned out to be her ex-boss, however, calling to discuss a freelance job he was sending out for her.

When she put the phone down, Marsh said, from his favourite reclining pose on the leather couch, 'Business?'

'That's a safe assumption.'

He shook his head sadly. 'I'm worried about you, Torey. There seem to be no hordes of old boyfriends begging you to come back to California——'

'That's what you think,' she said calmly. 'They all call in the daytime when you're at work. And as long as we're talking about a lack of phone calls, I'd think you'd be worried about yourself. Doesn't it occur to you that your Kimberley may have met a handsome Frenchman?'

'One she prefers to me?' Marsh sounded affronted. 'Of course not.'

'Well, there's no arguing with self-confidence,' Torey murmured.

'Oh, it isn't self-confidence. I trust that busload of senior citizens to keep her too busy to look. In the meantime, I'm far too busy thinking about the plumber.' And he went off, whistling and cheerful.

Torey had to admit that Marsh was at least maintaining a good-humoured attitude about the whole thing. She hadn't quite expected him to be the kind who tolerated delays—but then, the situation was easier for him than it was for her, she muttered in her less-than-patient moments.

She had a lot of those moments. Generally, the first one of the day occurred early in the morning, when she was jolted awake by the roar of the shower just on the other side of the wall at the head of her bed. It wasn't that Marsh had been so purposefully quiet that first day, she had learned to her regret; it was merely that she'd been too far away to hear all the noise he made.

In the last few days, it had been a different story. For one thing, he whistled. For another, he never varied the time of his morning shower by more than ten minutes, work-day or not. She had made that discovery on Sunday morning, to her displeasure. She had looked at the clock in horror and then had pulled the pillow over her head and cursed Marsh, Aunt Violet, her nurse, and plumbers in general until the splashing had stopped and she had finally been able to doze off again.

She had been giving serious thought to moving her bedroom once more, but on Thursday morning the plumber finally turned up, just as Torey wandered into the kitchen to find something for breakfast. If she had been slightly more awake, she would have greeted him with a few lines of the 'Hallelujah Chorus', but as it was she merely pointed to the stairs, gathered up an apple and a container of yoghurt, and retreated to her own room to work on the set of drawings for her ex-boss, which had finally come in yesterday's post.

At least, that was her intention, and despite the noise she did fairly well. Barely two hours later, she inked the last line of her drawing and put her pen down, then propped her elbows on the drawing-table and stared down at her work. From the heavy paper a shadowy-faced model in a suggestive pose and a slinky négligé looked back at her. Torey made a face at the sultry siren; this was the kind of work she hated most because there was so little room for originality in it.

'Don't complain,' she told herself. She picked up the pen and added a bit of shading to the folds of the négligé. 'It may not be your kind of art, but it certainly pays the grocery bill. And as for the kind of thing you'd rather be doing...'

'Admit it,' she told herself. 'You're still getting nowhere with the strip.'

A bang from the front of the house sent her pen skidding across the drawing, obliterating the model's face. Torey said a few words that were not a part of her usual vocabulary and went storming towards the front of the house to see what was going on. It had sounded as if the roof were falling in.

Not that I'm going to ask the plumber to keep the noise down, she told herself. It might slow up the job if he tried. But at least I can find out how long this is going to go on!

She stopped dead on the threshold of the master bathroom, blinking in surprise; there were two large males in there, and surely she remembered letting only one in the back door.

Then she recognised the larger and younger of the two. 'I thought you'd gone to work,' she accused.

'I have.' Marsh waved a hand around the room. 'You think this isn't work?' He was wearing old, tight-fitting jeans and a flannel shirt with the cuffs rolled to the elbows, and his dark hair had a coating of greyish dust. That, and the bang that had jolted her out of her chair, were easily explained, Torey concluded. There was now a gigantic hole in the tiled wall, as irregular and ragged as if they'd hit it with a sledgehammer.

She shivered at the idea, and for the first time began to calculate how long it might take to put this mess back together again. She didn't like the answers she was coming up with, so she said sweetly, 'Don't let me keep you from working. I'm going to go fix myself a cup of tea.'

Marsh's voice caught her as she crossed his bedroom. 'Uh—Torey——'

'I suppose you want one, too?'

'Not exactly. It's just that there's no water anywhere in the house. Sorry—I didn't think about saving some before Gus turned the main valve off in the cellar.'

It was amazing, Torey found, how one could go for hours on an ordinary day without ever running a tap, but as soon as the precious flow was cut off it was impossible to live without it. She couldn't even clean her pens—a tiresome job that she reserved for days like this when it was impossible to concentrate—because there was no water to rinse them.

'I'm going for a walk,' she called up the stairs, and without waiting for an answer she gathered up Stephanie Kendall's casserole dish and set out to find the footpath through the ravine. There were obligations one had to meet, she told herself. She'd been putting this one off for a week, waiting for Marsh to take care of it. But she was beginning to think she owed Stephanie thanks; Marsh seemed to have taken the woman's suggestions to heart, and he was being quite decent, all the way around. Except, of course, for the shower...

The path was easy enough to follow; it was a narrow, well-worn trail with stepping stones here and there when the way grew steep. It was warmer today, and the sky was bright, though not as brilliant as the California sunshine she was used to. The snow was almost gone now, and the grass was turning green, except in shaded corners where the sun did not go. The March wind was pleasantly gusty, bringing to her nose the aromas of cold soil and flowers just ready to burst into life.

The footpath led down to a tiny stream that rippled over a stony crossing and then up again to the backs of a row of houses, ending at the edge of the wooded area. Torey stopped in her tracks for a moment, staring at the huge, sprawling brick and stone house that was closest to the end of the footpath. Not the sort of place she had expected an estate agent to live in, she thought. Not in a town of this size, at any rate. Perhaps Stephanie had only meant that her house was near the end of the footpath.

But when she knocked at the back door to ask for directions, Stephanie herself answered.

'How many houses do you sell in the average week?' Torey asked without preface, eyeing the hand-hewn stone trim around the heavily carved door, and the golden oak kitchen that was visible over Stephanie's shoulder. 'Sorry—none of my business. The house just——'

'Startled you,' Stephanie agreed. 'I know—it's certainly not the average three-bedroom ranch, but we love it. Come in. I was hoping you'd drop in, and a little afraid that you might not.'

Torey shrugged, handed over the dish and said, 'There's no law against offering to buy something, is there? And you were only doing what Marsh wanted.'

'Still, I'm sorry. If I'd had any idea you didn't want to sell...' There was a gleam of understanding in the woman's eyes that for a second made Torey feel almost naked and eager to get away from the subject.

'I have to confess,' Torey said. 'I really came to beg a cup of tea. Between Marsh and the plumber, the house is impossible today.'

Stephanie smiled. 'I've had a few mornings like that. How is Marsh?' she asked over her shoulder as she went to put the kettle on. 'I haven't seen him for days.'

'He's been much more pleasant lately. He even laughed when he saw the nasty cartoon of him I'd drawn on my bedroom wall. Well, actually, it's *his* bedroom——' Then she swallowed hard and said weakly, 'That didn't come out quite the way I——'

'I'll take your word for it,' Stephanie said gravely, but there was a twinkle in her eyes. 'And your work? Is he leaving you alone?'

'He's been very co-operative. I gather I owe you thanks for that.'

Stephanie shrugged. 'I'm glad it worked out. I didn't really tell him anything, you know. He drew his own conclusions.' The words seemed to hover in the air, as if she was inviting Torey to confide in her. Then Stephanie pushed aside a neat stack of school papers and set a plate of brownies down between them, and the moment passed.

'Well, believe me, I'm grateful for the change,' Torey said. 'I thought for a while that we were going to fight over everything, right down to what size light bulb to use in the chandelier in the front hallway.'

'Well, I wouldn't advise letting your guard down, anyway. Marsh is a pretty decent sort, most of the time, but I've never seen him so super-sensitive over anything as he is about that house.'

'Oh? I'd have thought he was naturally the possessive sort.'

Stephanie shook her head. 'No. Not even over Kimberley, and I've heard some pretty catty things said about her in his presence.'

'There really is a Kimberley? I was beginning to think she was fictional!'

Stephanie laughed. 'Oh, no—she's real enough. She's from an old family here in Springhill, and her father was a partner in a business that went bankrupt some years ago and took the family fortunes on a nosedive. Personally I think Kimberley opened the travel agency just so she could continue the twice-annual trips to Europe and the winter vacations in Florida and the summer tours of Maine that she got used to when she was growing up.'

'I wonder where Marsh fits into that lifestyle.'

'As the credit card that funds it,' Stephanie said promptly. 'And that's one of the catty things I was talking about, because I'm the one who said it.' The kettle started to whistle, and she went to make the tea. 'I told him that Kimberley was getting tired of sharing her vacations with elderly ladies, and she was looking for an alternative and had settled on him.'

Torey wondered briefly how that fitted with what Marsh had told her about not being made of money. It would take more than just a decent income to stake the kind of travel Stephanie was talking about... None of your business, she told herself firmly. 'And it didn't bother him—what you'd said?'

'Marsh just laughed and asked if I wouldn't be a bit bored with it, too,' Stephanie said disgustedly and brought the teapot over to the table.

'I can't wait for her to get home,' Torey said thoughtfully.

Stephanie smiled. 'Well, that's one thing you and Marsh must have in common!' She handed Torey a mug. 'What I can't figure out is why Marsh is so set on having that house. He even came over here, you know, to ask me if there wasn't a way to force you to sign those papers.'

'That sounds like Marsh.'

'He didn't put it that way, of course, but that's what it came down to. I told him that since eminent domain did not apply, he was out of luck. But I still think it's odd that he should feel that way. I don't suppose he spent more than forty-eight hours in that house, total, all the years he was growing up.'

Torey sipped her tea and reached for a brownie. 'I gathered that there was a family falling-out.'

'One of the great scandals of Springhill. How well did you know your Aunt Violet?'

Torey shook her head. 'Not at all. She was my great-aunt, actually—my grandmother's sister—and they wrote to each other once in a while, but...'

'Well, of course it was before my time, but the story is that years ago Violet fell on hard times, and there was some comment now and then about her virtue because of the number of gentlemen who seemed to call on her. When she eloped with Vince Endicott less than two months after his wife died——'

'That was the scandal?' Torey asked weakly.

'Well, two months—it *was* awfully quick; you have to admit that. Marsh's father was among the people who felt that it wasn't just a matter of Vince's being lonely—he felt Violet had some sort of hold over his father, and he didn't hesitate to say what he thought.'

'No wonder Marsh didn't want to tell me what his father used to call her.'

'He didn't? You amaze me. None of the Endicotts spoke to each other for years. They patched it up eventually—Vince missed his grandson, and Marsh's father concluded that principles shouldn't stand in the way when you desperately need a job. So Ward went back to work for his father and eventually took over the business—Marsh runs it now, of course—but it was never what you'd call a warm and charming family.' She broke a brownie in half and took a thoughtful bite. 'If I were in Marsh's shoes, I'd never have set foot in that house again. I'd be afraid Violet would haunt me.'

'That's probably exactly why he's so determined—he wants to keep her from winning in the end.'

Stephanie looked across the table for a long moment. 'You understand him pretty well, don't you?' she said softly.

Torey was startled. Understand Marsh Endicott? No, she made no claims to that.

Stephanie didn't press the subject, to Torey's relief. 'You're coming to my party a week from Sunday, aren't you?'

The invitation had been in the morning's post—a welcome to spring, it had said. 'I'm not sure I can. I really should work.'

'On Sundays too? Is it going so well?'

'I wish it were. I keep getting packages from my old boss at the advertising agency. I'm glad to have the income, of course, but by the time I finish his projects I don't have any more time than I ever did for the strip.'

'I've always wondered how cartoonists kept it up, week after week.'

'I haven't had time to worry about that yet,' Torey admitted, and stopped herself from going on. What was there about this woman that made her want to confide all the details, to pour out the frustration of trying to make all the random ideas that floated through her head fit together into some sort of pattern?

The problem was that there were almost too many possibilities, and none of them seemed to fit together into the concept for an entire strip. Without that story-line, that single unifying theme, she would never have a true cartoon strip, but only a bunch of random, funny drawings. And, as far as that went, nothing she drew looked as funny any more as it used to...

It sounded so simple, this missing element, and perhaps, once she had discovered it, it would turn out to be uncomplicated. But finding it wasn't easy.

It would have to come from inside herself, that was sure. Everyone, she had found from long experience, had a sure-fire idea for a comic strip, and each was willing to share it with Torey. The problem was that most of the ideas were not only undeveloped and impossible to carry out, but also ill-suited to Torey's sense of humour. As a result, everyone ended up frustrated—the well-meaning, helpful friends who had volunteered their help, of course, but Torey most of all. That was why she had stopped talking to anyone about the possibility of a cartoon strip even before she had decided to come to Springhill.

And why I ever mentioned that damned thing to Stephanie, she thought wearily, is beyond me.

But Stephanie merely said, 'It's a completely different sort of work from any I've ever done, you see—the idea fascinates me. But surely if you try to work all the time, you'll fry your brain with the tension. You can't think creatively while you're under that sort of pressure.'

'Well——'

'Take Sunday afternoon off, at least, and come celebrate the first day of spring. It's a tradition.'

'I don't know,' Torey said uncertainly. 'I also don't like the idea of being too public around here just yet.'

'Because of you and Marsh and the house? Don't worry about it. It takes a lot more to make a scandal these days than it did in Violet's time, but the best way I know of to cause questions in Springhill is to act as if you have something to hide.'

Torey thought about that as she walked; she took the long way home, and stopped at the cemetery at the top of Oak Hill to see if the date of Violet's death had been carved on the granite headstone yet. It had; she stood beside the little heap of naked earth, staring at the garish whiteness of the new letters. They had carried out Violet's request, Stan had told her last weekend when he'd brought her over to visit the grave, by having no memorial services at all. Torey had thought the absence of ceremony a very odd thing to ask, but after hearing Stephanie's story this morning...

'Violet probably thought Marsh and his father would picket the church,' she muttered. 'And I'm not so sure but what she'd have been right!'

It was a beautiful day for a walk, the air crisp and fresh and invigorating. There was a different sort of feel to the air from anything Torey had ever experienced before, as if the refreshing zest of a carbonated beverage had somehow been added to the atmosphere. The breeze and the exercise made her feel better, and by the time she reached Main Street, Torey had decided that Stephanie was right. If she was going to be a resident of Springhill, then she might as well start getting to know people. Mrs Moore across the street wasn't the only person who was watching and wondering. And, as Stephanie had said, to keep to oneself was to invite comment.

So when Stan Spaulding hailed her on the street and asked if she would go to a banquet with him on Saturday night, she accepted without another thought. All work and no play *did* make a dull girl—one who found it hard to see humour in anything.

The change of attitude seemed to have helped already, she thought a half-hour later, back in her room, as she finished a drawing of a plumber brandishing a wrench at a harried couple who were tied to a pipe. 'A new form of water torture,' she lettered neatly across the bottom, and tossed it into a basket that stood on the corner of her bed. It was a decent cartoon that still fitted nowhere into a strip, she reflected, but at least she had finished something.

Marsh poked his head around the door-jamb. 'You *are* here,' he said, as if surprised. 'I thought for a while you were never coming back.'

'And you were delighted by the idea, right?' Torey didn't raise her head from the new page she was lining up on the board.

He came across the room. 'I hadn't thought of it that way. We still have no water——'

'I noticed.'

'Gus got called off to an emergency, so I thought——'

Torey laid her pencil down and looked up at him, eyes narrowed. 'Emergency? And our situation isn't an emergency.'

'Broken water pipe. We've got no water, but they've got too much. He'll be back as soon as he gets the flood fixed. In the meantime I thought I'd take you out to lunch. Sort of an apology for messing up your day.'

'Gus is the one who should apologise. Don't tell me— I can hear him.' Her pencil flew across the page, and Gus the plumber came to life, his gloomy, hangdog expression peering out from the paper. She tossed it at Marsh. 'The caption is, "I can't get your water pipes working again till tomorrow," the plumber said drily.'

Marsh groaned. 'If you're going to behave like that, perhaps I should reconsider my invitation to lunch.' He glanced at the drawing and then reached for the one in the basket and held it up at arm's length. 'Still—I did offer, and my mother taught me it wasn't polite to take back an invitation. How about it?'

'Why?' Torey asked crisply. 'Do you have another scheme you want to try out on me?'

'No—I thought I'd build up some credit for being a nice guy.'

'Too late.' But she smiled when she said it. 'Sure— I'd love to have lunch with you.'

He swept her a graceful bow. 'I am honoured, Miss Farrell,' he murmured.

She pretended not to have heard. 'Despite the company, it will be much more pleasant than eating soup from the can, with no water to dilute it.'

'You can say that again. How about a truce for the duration?'

It was the first time she'd ever been in his car, a small, bright red, sporty model that she suspected could travel just about as fast as the average rocket. 'Nice,' she said, sinking into the leather seat. 'I could covet this car. Mine just doesn't want to run right these days—it keeps dying at inappropriate times. But then, my drawing-board wouldn't fit in the back seat of this one very well, would it?'

'Why worry about the drawing-board? Are you planning to go somewhere?' Marsh asked, with bright-eyed interest.

Tory laughed. 'Nope. I like it here, now that it's starting to warm up.'

'It won't last.'

'But spring starts next week!'

'According to the calendar, perhaps. But it's likely to snow again.'

'Actually, that sounds like fun,' she said dreamily.

'You'll think so the first time you have to shovel the driveway.'

'Only my half,' she murmured, and gave him her sweetest smile.

He took her to a service station at the edge of town. Torey had seen it from the highway; it was a big metal shed that looked as if it should have housed a tractor showroom instead of a restaurant. She almost commented about his apparent desire to keep her hidden away, but then she remembered the truce he had proposed, and swallowed the tart comment.

He seemed to have read her mind, anyway. 'They've got the best apple pie in town,' he said earnestly.

Inside, the restaurant was warm and cosy, with fresh jonquils on the tables. Before they had even sat down, Marsh's coffee-cup was full and the pot was half tipped over Torey's cup as the waitress asked, 'Coffee, miss?'

She nodded. 'Do you come here often, Marsh?' she asked innocently as she stirred the dark, fragrant liquid.

'No more than twice a day,' he drawled. 'The plant is right across the road, so it's handy.'

She had seen the sprawling complex of warehouses as they had turned off the highway, but she hadn't known what it was. 'You run that whole thing? I thought——' She stopped abruptly.

'That whole thing,' he agreed gently. 'We do business in twelve states and Canada.'

'And you still can't get a plumber in less than a week?' Torey took a hasty sip of coffee, burning her mouth. 'Sorry, Marsh.'

He gave the waitress their order and sat back, his coffee-cup cradled in one hand.

'Can I ask you a question?' she asked.

He raised one silky eyebrow, and Torey went on, firmly, 'A serious one, I mean. Did you honestly expect the house to be this much trouble?'

Marsh sighed and set his cup down. 'Of course I did. It's an old house. What I didn't expect was how crazy it would be to have to live in the middle of the mess. But I couldn't turn down the chance to sell my town house.'

'Don't you miss it?' she asked, genuinely curious.

He gave her a crooked smile. 'Only the plumbing. I always knew what to expect. But otherwise——' He shook his head. 'It was a pretty typical new construction. Walls like wrapping paper, floors that bounced—you know the sort of thing. It was fine for a while, but old houses have a personality, Torey, that makes up for their charming unreliability. It's like snuggling down into a toasty-warm blanket.'

'And then getting an ice cube down your back the moment you've gotten comfortable.'

'Something like that. And the work has only started.'

She sighed. 'I suppose that's just another way of telling me that I should be realistic and turn the house over to you.' It was supposed to be a challenge; instead it came out soft and wistful.

'What other options do you have?' It was kind enough. 'Unless you're expecting some other great-aunt to die and leave you a fortune.'

Torey shook her head morosely. 'I'm all out of aunts.'

'Are you really as alone as you seem to be, Torey?'

She looked up in surprise over the rim of her coffee-cup. 'What makes you say that?'

He shrugged. 'The lack of phone calls. No personal mail.'

'Are you spying on me?' It was out before she realised that to say it was to confirm the basic truth of his deduction. She darted a wary glance at him. But he didn't seem pleased to have his suspicions confirmed. He just looked at her, with something in his dark eyes that seemed to draw the truth from her before she even realised she was speaking.

'My parents died when I was little,' she said slowly, 'and my grandmother raised me. She was very special and loving and gentle, but she was often ill, and I didn't like to leave her alone. So I guess I just didn't have a lot of time for friends. And then when Gran died last year—well, other things were more important.'

Things like cartoon strips, she thought, and chasing dreams... But those things were none of Marsh's business. 'Gran was Violet's sister, you know,' she added briskly. 'I've always wondered if they were alike.'

'No.' It was bald, and firm, and harsh.

Torey looked at him in surprise. 'What was Violet like, Marsh?'

'Not the sort to inspire devotion,' he said crisply. 'Beyond that, I really couldn't say—I saw so little of her. But we were talking about the house, Torey. You're going to have to give up this game soon, anyway.'

'You'll see.'

He let the silence drag out for a long moment. 'I deduce that you're talking about this special project of yours, Torey.'

'That's right.'

'But I thought,' he said softly, 'that was going to be your ticket out of Springhill—not what would let you afford to stay.'

For a moment, she had completely forgotten the story that had allowed her to have this week of peaceful co-operation. Torey could have bitten her wayward tongue off at the roots. That was what happened when one got all soft and sentimental!

'Perhaps you'd better tell me more about it,' he said. There was a thread of steel under the casual suggestion. 'You aren't just an ordinary freelance commercial artist, are you, Victoria?'

What difference did it make if she told him? she asked herself. He was probably already plotting how to make up for the time he had lost, how to make her life miserable in as many different ways as he could devise. But perhaps if he knew what she was really doing he might concentrate on that, and if he didn't destroy every single minute she'd still have a fighting chance, at least . . .

'No, I'm not just a commercial artist,' she said coolly. 'By the first day of June, I'll have produced thirteen weeks' worth of a new cartoon strip. A syndicate in California has already agreed to offer it nationwide.' She crossed her fingers under the table. If they like it, she added silently. Well, they would like it. They had to.

He whistled, softly. 'Thereby giving you not only fame but fortune—right?'

'You've got it.'

'And you plan to pour it into the house?'

'I might.'

'What's the strip about?'

She looked straight at him and told the absolute truth, knowing that he would not believe it. 'I haven't the vaguest idea.'

His laugh started in his eyes, she thought absently, with a sort of glow in the dark depths. Then the tiny lines at the corners of his eyes crinkled together, and the corners of his mouth quirked, and finally he threw himself back in his chair with an explosion of laughter that drew attention from every table in the building.

'Please Marsh—everybody is looking,' she said, and was not consoled by this proof that he had not been trying to hide her after all. How many of these people were his employees? she wondered. There would certainly be a new topic of conversation at the plant this afternoon; they couldn't ignore this!

He sat up and pulled a white handkerchief from his back pocket and mopped his eyes. 'It just struck me as funny,' he said.

'I gathered that.'

'What's it really about, Torey? A city girl who inherits a hog farm or something? And you're here in Springhill because you need to do research—right?'

'Honestly, Marsh . . .'

The waitress brought their cheeseburgers. Marsh spread ketchup across the top of his bun and mused, 'A California syndicate—it has to be something completely off the wall, or they wouldn't find it humorous. I know—it involves one of those incredible religions they keep hatching out there.'

'Not everyone in California belongs to a cult, Marsh. I'm sure you don't appreciate it when people on the West Coast don't bother to find out that Iowa isn't all flat and square——'

'Don't try to change the subject; I don't get distracted easily. I'll get the right idea sooner or later.' He frowned at his cheeseburger, spread the pickles neatly across the top of it, gathered it up and took a bite. 'Even if it takes me till the first of June.'

That makes two of us who have made that pledge, Torey thought sombrely. I wonder which of us will give up first.

CHAPTER FIVE

THE waste-paper basket at Torey's feet was full again by Saturday afternoon, and crumpled pages had over-flowed into the cramped space between the drawing-table and her bed. She would have emptied the whole mess into the dustbin by the back door if it had not been for Marsh. He hadn't said anything more about her cartoon strip since their lunch together, but she didn't think he had stopped speculating. And, while she didn't think he would barge into her bedroom to spy, she suspected that he would feel no compunction about looking through the rubbish. And she had no intention of letting him guess that she was still at a loss herself. Ten days of struggling and sketching and doodling and thinking and pacing, and what did she have to show for it? The over-flowing waste-paper basket and a stock of drawing-paper which was going steadily and ominously downhill.

She rubbed her tired eyes and yawned and pulled her baggy sweater over her head. She was tired of living in sweat-suits and jeans, she decided; it would be nice to dress up for a change, and go out to dinner with a young man.

She smiled wryly to herself. And perhaps, she thought, after a hot shower, I might even believe that!

It was true enough, if only she weren't so tired. She liked Stan Spaulding, and she enjoyed spending time with him. But tonight, she'd rather just curl up with a bowl of salted peanuts and a mindless television show...

You're not tired, she diagnosed herself. You're de-pressed, and the worst thing you could do would be to stay home and feel sorry for yourself. At any rate, she had promised Stan that she would go to this dinner tonight. The annual banquet for the local community threatre group... She yawned again. It wasn't likely to be the Academy Awards, that was certain.

She could almost hear what Marsh would have to say if she'd had the bad sense to voice that opinion. 'Longing for the lure of the city?' he would say, with feigned sympathy. 'What a shame that you're stuck here. Perhaps we could arrange something...'

She was just reaching for her terry robe when she heard the rush of water in the bathroom next door. She glanced at the clock and groaned. It was just like Marsh, she thought, to have awakened her this morning at an unconscionable time for a Saturday, and to be in the shower again now, when she was expecting Stan to pick her up in less than an hour. Could the man actually read her mind and figure out how to be the most annoying, while continuing to look innocent? She wouldn't put it past him.

She banged on the bathroom door and shouted, 'Must you always be in the shower, Marsh?'

'Would you rather I ran around tracking dust all over the house?' His voice was a bit muffled by the hiss of the water.

'What sort of dust? Did you actually clean something?'

'Not exactly. I've been working in that damned bathroom all day.'

'Gus doesn't work on Saturdays,' she reminded crisply. 'And you told me that you don't do plumbing.'

'I don't. And I'm not a carpenter, either, but it doesn't take much skill to rip out a rotted floor.'

'Rotted—you're joking. If Violet never used the water——'

'I didn't say she *never* did. Some time in the last forty years something leaked, and the floor's been going quietly to pieces ever since. We just found it yesterday when we took the tub out.'

'Took it *out*?' Tory squeaked. 'Why——?'

'It's a good thing you didn't get that tub full of water, by the way—with the added weight, it would probably have come straight through the dining-room ceiling with you in it.'

The image which that evoked tickled her fancy, and she giggled, in spite of herself. 'That would have been an even better scene.'

There was an answering chuckle from the other side of the door. 'Come to think of it, it would have been worth seeing the look on Stephanie's face.'

It annoyed her; she wasn't quite sure why. 'Sorry to disappoint you,' she said curtly, 'but it still wouldn't have sent me back to Los Angeles screaming. When are you going to be out of there, Marsh?'

'When the hot water stops feeling so wonderful against my sore back.'

'I have a date. And I don't like cold showers.'

'So come on in while it's hot. My mother taught me to share.'

It took a moment for Torey to find her voice. 'My goodness, you are missing Kimberley, aren't you? Well, tap on my door—no, don't bother. I'll know when you're finished.'

The rush of water died. 'Does that mean the noise bothers you?'

Torey sighed and cursed her runaway tongue. Now the man would probably spend all his free time in the shower...

The door opened abruptly, and Torey's eyes widened in surprise. Marsh was wearing a towel casually knotted around his waist, and he was rubbing his hair with another. Water was still beaded up on his tanned skin; it had gathered on his eyelashes, and it dripped from the neat little ringlets of dark hair on his broad chest. She only realised that she was staring when he raised one eyebrow at her and said, 'You look shocked.'

'I didn't expect——' She reasserted her self-control with an effort and added, 'You're dripping all over the floor. What are you trying to do, rot this one too?'

'I thought you wanted me to hurry so I could be waiting by the front door to make polite conversation with your date while you finish making yourself beautiful.'

'Must you make it sound as if it's going to take countless hours, Marsh?' And why, she asked herself, should a question she had intended to sound cynical have come out in an almost wistful tone?

He half smiled. 'I didn't mean that, exactly. But you will have to scrub the ink off your eyelid. It looks as if I belted you, and I can't allow you to go out in public like that, I'm afraid. My reputation...' He touched the tender skin at the corner of her eye with a wet fingertip.

It felt cold, and Torey shivered and ducked away, turning to check her image in the steamed-up mirror. He was right about the ink. 'So why don't you go away so I can start scrubbing? And, by the way, I do not want you to greet my date at the door.'

'Who are you going out with, anyway?'

If he couldn't figure it out all by himself, Torey saw no reason to tell him. So she ignored the question and put a hand in the middle of his back to urge him out of the door. His skin was smooth and slick and cool to the touch.

She hurried to get under the hot spray. She was going to make sure, even if it killed her, that she would be waiting inside the front door when the bell rang so that Marsh would have no excuse to answer it.

She didn't make it. She was still tipping her eyelashes with mascara and cursing the fate that had made them blonde and almost invisible, instead of black and thick and curly like Marsh's were—'And just when,' she asked herself curtly, 'have you had time for such an exhaustive study of the man's eyelashes?'—when the doorbell sounded. She swore under her breath, grabbed for the pale blue wool jersey dress that lay across her bed, stepped into her shoes and started down the stairs, tugging the hemline into place with one hand and pulling at the zipper with the other.

The carillon hadn't even finished playing yet when she reached the bottom step, but she was too late. Marsh had already opened the door, and a tall, trouser-clad figure was framed against the dying twilight.

'Dammit, Marsh,' she said. 'I asked you not to——'

Then she realised that this was not the lanky, cheerfully smiling man she had expected. Instead, a slender, olive-skinned woman stepped across the threshold.

'I just got off the plane,' she said in a deep, throaty voice. 'And I've already heard the most appalling rumours about you, Marsh. Am I hallucinating from jet lag, or have you actually moved into Violet Endicott's house?' She turned to stare at Torey. 'And this must be the blonde—woman—the gossips say you're sharing the place with. Would you care to introduce me to your little friend, Marsh, darling?'

If Kimberley Cameron was actually suffering from jet lag, Torey thought resentfully, the cosmetics companies were missing a sure bet; they should bottle the stuff and sell it as a beauty aid. The woman looked as if she had just stepped off a modelling runway, not an airport one; every French-braided brunette hair was in place, her tweed trouser-suit looked as if it had been steam-pressed, and her make-up was as fresh as if she'd come from a professional salon within the last half-hour.

Torey shook herself a bit and murmured an excuse. As she climbed the stairs to finish her mascara, she heard that disastrously clear and throaty voice say, 'Aren't you going to kiss me, Marsh, dear? I must admit the stories took me by surprise, but now that I've actually met her—well——'

It was exactly what Marsh had implied; Kimberley would understand because there was nothing about Torey that could possibly make her feel threatened. It left Torey feeling just a little sick. She thought, No wonder Marsh said it would take me hours to be beautiful. I could work all the hours of the week and I still couldn't look like that . . .

She knew it was bad manners, but she couldn't stop herself from peering over the railing at the top of the stairs, just in time to see the most restrained kiss she'd ever witnessed—except, she decided, for an old B-grade movie. She wanted to call downstairs and tell them not to be concerned about her presence, that she was not cut out to be a chaperon. Instead, she went on up to her room and closed her door—as loudly as she could without slamming it, so that they would get the message.

If it had been me, she thought, and I hadn't seen the man I loved for three weeks, I'd have grabbed him and held him and kissed him till neither of us could breathe any longer.

She put her elbows on the top of her tiny dressing-table and stared into her make-up mirror. If it had been me, she thought dreamily, I wouldn't have cared who was there watching.

She stirred, uneasily, disturbed by the mental image of a tall, dark-haired man returning bear-hug for bear-hug, kiss for kiss, until she was too dizzy to stand by herself . . .

It took her by surprise; there had been men in her life, of course, but never anyone who had inspired that sort of imaginative longing. Her relationships had been casual, friendly ones—there hadn't been time for anything else to grow, between Gran's needs and her own devotion to her dreams. Oh, there had been one or two that could have gone further, if she had allowed it. One of them had implied that he might propose, if she would only be sensible, give up this silly pipe-dream of a cartoon strip and settle down to her perfectly good job in commercial art. She had liked him a great deal, but not as much as she loved her drawing, and though it had been a wrench to say goodbye, she had not missed him for long. Some day, she had told herself, there would be a man who understood...

And that, she told herself briskly, had nothing to do with this sudden fantasy of standing on a street corner somewhere kissing a man without concern for who might be passing by!

Marsh and Kimberley were coming up the stairs as she started down to wait for Stan. Torey stepped off to the corner of the upstairs hall and did her best to become invisible. It wasn't hard; Marsh was watching Kimberley as if every breath she took were a fascinating new discovery, and Kimberley was eyeing the vintage art deco light fixture at the top of the stairs. Torey wasn't sure if the woman's look was covetous or shocked, but she resented it no matter what; she'd spent hours just yesterday working off nervous energy by polishing that light.

They went straight to the master bedroom, and Torey fought down an embarrassed blush and hurried down the first flight of stairs. After all, it was none of her business what consenting adults did in the privacy of their homes, and she couldn't exactly argue about whether Marsh had a right to bring a guest to that bedroom.

Nevertheless, she hoped Stan wouldn't be late.

She had just started down the second flight when Kimberley shrieked, and Torey lost her footing and had to grab for the railing.

'Good lord,' Kimberley said, very firmly. 'Marsh, you have got to be joking. I concede that the downstairs has a certain charm, and with the right wallpaper and furniture—but Marsh, darling, this is primitive! I could cry at the idea of living here, when we could build a *nice* house—our *own* house——'

'Hear, hear,' Torey muttered. 'That's my girl. Get him out of this house, Kimberley, and you'll be my friend for life!'

She heard Marsh's voice rise and fall. It was a soothing tone, but she could only make out an occasional word. 'Fireplace,' she thought she heard him say once, and the throaty answer confirmed it.

'They still build fireplaces now, you know,' Kimberley said sharply. 'Quite nice ones, actually!'

Torey was waiting, with her coat already on, when Stan arrived. He looked a little surprised when she stepped outside rather than inviting him in, and he said, 'We've got plenty of time. Besides, I need to ask Marsh about something.'

Torey shook her head firmly. 'I think it would be better right now to leave the love-birds to their nesting negotiations.'

He frowned. 'Oh. You mean Kimberley's back.'

'And she hates the house.'

'I thought she might. I tried to tell Marsh that before he moved in, but he wouldn't listen.'

'Does he ever?' Torey asked.

'To Kimberley—perhaps.'

It was only a few blocks to the sprawling hotel where the banquet was being held. Torey was silently thoughtful for most of the way, and it was only as Stan was parking the car that she asked, 'Stan, what happens to me if Marsh moves out? Legally, I mean? I can't buy his half; I can't afford it. And I won't sell mine.'

Stan shrugged. 'I doubt he'll give it up so easily.'

'For Kimberley?' Torey asked softly.

'Well—perhaps you're right. But even if he decides to sell, as Marsh himself so correctly pointed out, who on earth is going to buy half a house?'

She laughed; she couldn't help it. It was one of the things she liked best about Stan, this kinship that came over them at odd moments when they had to deal with Marsh's eccentricities. But she also couldn't help remembering Marsh's threat to file a lawsuit against her and force the sale of the house. And she knew that Stan was very carefully refraining from reminding her of that possibility.

The community theatre group was small, but the noise was out of all proportion to the number of people gathered in the banquet room. Torey felt like a sparrow among a bunch of cardinals and jays; her pale blue dress faded into insignificance against the costume—there was no other word—which many of the other women were wearing.

She was still looking over the crowd when Stan tensed beside her. 'Damn,' he muttered. 'What are they doing here? They're not theatre people at all.'

'Who?' But she couldn't see who he was watching, and a moment later, when a middle-aged woman in a vintage Charleston dress and feathered headband came up and introduced herself, Torey forgot about it.

'I'm president of The Players this year,' the woman announced, 'and I'm always recruiting new members. Stan tells me you're an artist, and that you do wonderful work. What kind? Scenery? Signs? Programmes? I can keep naming possibilities all night, you know, till you volunteer for something!' She drew Torey off to join a group, announcing loudly that she had a new trophy to introduce. Torey didn't even see Stan again till dinner, when he appeared beside her and muttered, 'Sorry. I tried, but I couldn't get us out of it.'

'Out of what?' Torey asked distractedly, but he didn't answer, just guided her to a table for four, held her chair, and threw himself down next to her as if he were expecting the acoustical tile above their heads to fall on him at any moment.

Across from Torey, a woman in her late fifties, in a simple, tailored black shirt-dress with a row of perfectly matched pearls peeking out from the open collar, smiled at her. 'You're new in town, aren't you?' she asked. 'I don't think we've met.'

Torey returned the smile. 'I haven't had time to meet anyone, really,' she said. Her gaze strayed to the woman's companion, sitting beside her. 'I've only been here for a few——'

She couldn't help it; the Farrell Searchlight, that habit of assessing each face she saw, of surveying each feature and deciding how it could best be caricatured, was too old and ingrained a practice to be easily broken. And when she was reminded of patterns she had seen in another face, at some other time, she was always fascinated until she had traced down the resemblance in her memory.

This face was lined with good humour and years, and the man's hair was pure spun-silver. But the deep-set dark eyes, and the shape of the nose, and the strength of the chin—there was no doubt in her mind where she had seen those things before. This was what Marsh would look like when he was sixty.

'I'm Dolores Endicott,' the woman said, and put out a slim hand. 'This is my husband, Ward.'

Torey shot an accusing glance at Stan, who only nodded miserably, tugged on his moustache, and mouthed, 'Sorry. I told you I tried to get us out of it.'

'It was inevitable,' Stan said. He took both hands off the steering-wheel to make a gesture of hopelessness. 'This is not exactly a metropolis, you know, and the Endicotts are pretty prominent. Marsh runs that business, but his father still takes a very active interest in it. And Dolores belongs to everything.'

'Except The Players, I thought you said,' Torey muttered. She didn't even turn her head to look at him.

'Well, how was I to know she'd joined? Anyway, you'd have run into them somewhere before long. At the supermarket, if nothing else. Though, come to think of it, maybe Marsh hasn't even told them about you.'

'Even if Marsh hasn't,' Torey said gloomily, 'someone else would have taken delight in sharing the news.'

'But Dolores didn't seem to recognise your name——'

'She didn't make a scene,' Torey corrected. 'There's a difference. Just because she didn't start screaming and frothing at the mouth when I told her who I was...'

He apparently wasn't listening. 'And Ward seemed to genuinely like you.'

'Obviously Ward has mellowed since the days when he used to call Aunt Violet——' she paused and frowned '—whatever it was he called her. Marsh never did exactly tell me.' She stopped abruptly and stared at Stan. 'Why are you so worried about it, anyway? If you've suddenly realised that being seen with me might ruin your image, perhaps you'd better take me straight home. Or you could drop me off right here and I'll creep along in the dark shadows——'

'Don't be ridiculous, Torey.'

There was a brief, strained silence, and then Torey sighed. 'I'm sorry, Stan. It was an awful thing to say, when you've stood up for me to Marsh, and risked losing his friendship over me.'

He parked the car in front of the house on Belle Vista and came around to open her door. 'You've just been pushing yourself too hard,' he diagnosed. 'I know you're under a lot of strain, Torey.'

That made her feel even smaller. He walked her up to the veranda, and at the front door she turned and said, 'I'd invite you in, but—the love-birds, you know...'

'You mean Marsh and Kimberley? Do you really think...?'

'Well, she *has* been gone a long time,' Torey said primly.

Stan smiled wryly. 'I'm beginning to hold a grudge against my old friend Marsh.' He kissed her lightly on the mouth, looked down at her for a long moment, and was gone into the night.

The house was dark, but the flicker of a dying fire in the big parlour threw shifting shadows across the patterned floor in the hallway. Torey hung her coat in the hall cupboard and went to stand in the arched doorway of the parlour. Only embers were left in the grate, angry, orange-red coals that seemed to vibrate with the intense heat inside them. It must have been quite a fire, Torey thought, and wondered if it had featured champagne and caviare and a blanket on the hearth and two people who had missed each other...

Something moved, startling her into immobility, and a dark head appeared over the back of the white leather couch. 'Torey?'

'Sorry, Marsh,' she said, very quickly. 'I was just on my way up the stairs. I didn't mean to intrude——' Stop babbling, she told herself. He's the one that should be embarrassed, not you.

He rose and went over to the fireplace. 'The only thing you're intruding on is my nap.' He poked at the embers and added a small log; the fire flared and the light fell harshly across his chiselled face. 'And since I really didn't intend to fall asleep on the couch... Your lipstick is smudged, by the way.'

She put a hand automatically to her mouth. 'In this light, how can you tell? The eyes of experience, no doubt.' She darted a glance at the couch. That's stupid, she told herself. What do you expect, that he'd have slid Kimberley underneath the cushions to conceal her?

Actually, it looked as if the woman hadn't been there at all. There was only a single glass on the coffee-table, and it was not a champagne flute; it looked more as if he'd been drinking ginger ale. Beside it was a garishly jacketed book, a hardback thriller called *The Facts Of Death*, with a marker about a third of the way through.

He seemed to read her mind. 'It was a very exciting Saturday night,' he said. 'Kimberley went home to sleep off her jet lag.'

'You have my deepest sympathy,' Torey murmured. She reached for a tissue from the box on the coffee-table and wiped her lips. 'How's that?'

He made a noise that might have been grudging approval. She glanced at him, half irritated—she didn't have to repair her lipstick to please him, after all!—and was startled to find him watching her closely, with something in his dark eyes that defied description.

Whatever it is he's gathering his courage to say, she thought, I'll bet I'm not going to like it. But I'd better give him the opportunity.

She perched on the very edge of the couch and picked up his book, just to have something to do with her hands. 'I'm amazed you could fall asleep at all, if you've been reading this sort of thing, Marsh.'

He put another log on the fire and sat down on the
far end of the couch, his body turned at an angle so that
he could watch her profile. She shifted nervously, and
then told herself not to be a fool. After all, the couch
and the coffee-table were the only two pieces of furniture in the room; she could hardly expect him to sit
on the floor just because she'd rather he kept his
distance!

But when he spoke, it wasn't at all what she had
expected. 'Did you and Stan enjoy the awards banquet?'

So he *had* known where she was going, and the man
she was with. 'It was wonderful,' Torey said crisply.
'Your parents were given the president's award for service
to The Players, by the way. Something about a stunning
contribution to the fund for a new theatre.'

He nodded, as if it didn't surprise him. 'And of course
you met them.'

'Don't think I engineered it! I had no idea.'

He didn't seem to be listening. 'We're going to have
to work this out, Torey. It can't go on.'

'Oh?' She twisted around to face him. 'Does that mean
you were wrong about Kimberley's reaction? Didn't she
relish the idea of all of us living here cosily like The
Three Musketeers after all?'

'Torey, you're being irrational.'

She thought, I am tired of being dismissed as a foolish
little girl! Stan had done the same thing tonight, and this
was the last straw.

'Am I?' she asked silkily. 'Are you certain that it's
not you who isn't seeing things quite straight, Marsh?
Not that I'm any competition for Kimberley, of course,
we all know that. Or do we? There are men who find
me attractive, you know. Perhaps Kimberley knows that,
too...' She slid sensuously to her feet and walked around
behind the couch, trailing her fingertips lightly across

the shoulder-seams of his charcoal-grey sweater. 'I've never really tried being nice to you——'

He shifted uneasily. 'Torey——'

'Are you afraid?' she asked, in a purring whisper. Her palms caressed the soft wool, and the muscular flesh under it seemed to quiver. She smiled a little. 'Afraid of me—Marsh?'

He looked up at her, his dark eyes unreadable in the dim room. 'What the hell are you trying to prove, Victoria?'

She couldn't answer. Something inside her seemed to flinch in disgust at her own flaunting behaviour. Stop it, Torey, she told herself. You're acting like a perfect fool! But she couldn't seem to move—her hands were apparently stuck to his sweater.

He removed them gently, his fingers closing around her wrists to lift the weight of her hands from his shoulders. She almost thanked him.

Then, in an instant, his hands slid upward, and the gentle grip on her wrists became a crushing grasp on her upper arms. She was already off balance because of the way she had been leaning over him, and so she was no match for the sudden tug that pulled her off her feet and over the back of the couch to land awkwardly on top of him. One arm was twisted under her breasts, and she desperately tried to raise herself, to stay an inch or two away from him.

She couldn't do it. The little oxygen that hadn't been driven from her lungs by the impact had seemed to freeze; she couldn't even gasp for breath, much less struggle when he captured her wrist and drew the last obstacle from between them, so that her breasts were crushed against his chest and her own weight held her hostage. His hands roamed casually across her shoulder-blades and down over her spine, pressing her even closer against the heat of his body, shifting her until his lips brushed hers.

His mouth was searing, and the shock of the contact drained the little strength she had left. She felt herself melting against him; her hair swung wildly across his face and he pushed it back untidily, cupping the back of her head with one large hand to hold the blonde mass out of his way. He kissed her greedily, his tongue probing, plundering, and Torey answered gladly, savouring the taste of him, the scent of his soap, the way her body fitted so pleasantly against his...

I knew it would be like this, she thought dizzily, and then a wave of disgust swept over her like a bucket of icy water—disgust at her own behaviour.

I wasn't trying to get even because he said I was being irrational, she thought wearily. *I didn't even have a principle to prove, not really. I provoked him because I wanted to find out what it would be like to have him kiss me...*

CHAPTER SIX

TOREY'S hands were under Marsh's head, palms up, against the leather cushion, her fingertips caressing the sensual silkiness of his hair. She dragged her unwilling fingers away from the softness, braced her palms against the cushion and pushed as hard as she could. His grip had slackened to a gentle, more persuasive kind of touch, and Torey had no trouble breaking free. She found herself sprawling on the floor beside the couch, her skirt in a tangle around her hips, her hair over her face, her eyes burning with hot, bitter tears.

Marsh said thickly, 'Would you mind telling me what hit you?'

She didn't answer. What could she possibly say, anyway? He would never believe the truth, that she was so disgusted with herself that she would cheerfully go and jump off the roof just now rather than face herself in a mirror. She had asked for it, after all.

And, because she had invited that sort of behaviour, he would also never believe that she was even more disgusted with him than with herself. She was almost sick to her stomach, in fact. What kind of a man would conduct himself like that—kiss and hold and almost make love to one woman, when he had given his pledge to another?

There is no justification for what he has done, she thought wearily. He can't even plead that loneliness for his absent fiancée drove him over the brink! Not that I would consider *that* as just cause, either.

'Sorry,' he said heavily. He hauled himself up from the couch, poked at the fire, and then stood staring down at it with his back turned to her.

Torey wasn't sure if she could stand up without shaking, so she settled for pushing herself into a sitting position with her spine propped against the front of the couch. She rubbed her elbow moodily; it was throbbing from the abrupt contact with the hardwood floor.

'I'd say you're right,' Marsh said. 'Some men do find you attractive. I'm among them.'

'I'm not flattered.' It was curt.

He turned then. 'Torey—it was a bad attempt at a joke, all right?'

A joke? That's understandable enough, she thought. I must look like a dust mop that's been held out the door and shaken. Not at all as Kimberley looks——

'I'm very sorry.' He held out his hands in a gesture that was almost pleading.

She wanted to let him touch her again, to hold her and caress her. She wanted to let her hands wander over his body, too, to toy with his hair, which really was as soft as it looked——

He took two quick steps towards her, and she pushed herself up from the floor, feeling something that was almost blind panic, and ran across the hallway and up the stairs. She didn't admit even to herself, until she was safely in her own room and leaning against the closed door, that she had not run because she was afraid of him—but because she was afraid of herself.

She let her head fall back against the door, feeling suddenly too exhausted to hold herself upright. Her hands were clenched together behind her back and pressed against the solid wood panel, and she was breathing in desperate little gasps.

But it was not the exertion of her dash up the stairs that was causing this discomfort now. This was an ache of the soul when forced to confront a truth she would much rather have ignored.

But she no longer could pretend. Marsh had kissed her, and nothing would ever be the same again. Despite her disgust for a man who could behave like that, she could not deny the attraction she felt for him. It was that attraction that had been working on her earlier. When she had imagined losing herself in a man's embrace, it had been Marsh she was dreaming of.

And, she admitted wearily, if she hadn't left the room when she did—if she had stayed there and allowed him to touch her again, let herself feel the man's magnetism again—anything might have happened. Anything at all.

And what if he had not wanted to touch her again? What if he had been coming towards her to comfort her, to apologise and then to send her safely off to bed?

That, she freely admitted, would have been even worse.

She didn't see him at all on Sunday; he was gone by the time she ventured from her room in the morning. She was relieved at first, and then apprehensive.

'This is ridiculous,' she told herself firmly as she created an omelette for her lunch. 'You're shying from shadows, making it more important than it was. Certainly he's an attractive man, but that doesn't mean you've gone permanently crazy over him. You've been living in awkward circumstances, that's all. You've seen him in a towel; you'd have to be blind not to find him attractive.'

She took a deep breath and continued the lecture. 'As for last night, you said some incredibly dumb things; the man seized an opportunity to get even, and things got a bit out of hand. That's all there is to it. You don't have to worry about it happening again, because it obviously shook him up just as much as it did you—he didn't expect that sort of reaction from either of us. To make it out as some sort of big deal would be the stupidest thing you ever did, Torey Farrell. After all, it was only a kiss. Treat it casually.'

But how was she to treat it casually—or any other way at all—if Marsh was nowhere to be seen?

And had he left the house because he was doing his best to stay away from Torey, or simply because he wanted to spend the day with Kimberley, now that she'd had a chance to vanquish her jet lag?

'Don't start imagining things,' she told herself sternly. 'Like believing that you're important enough to influence anything he does.'

Stan dropped by in the late afternoon; they ordered a pizza and built a fire and sat on the floor in front of the hearth to eat. Stan looked a little woefully at the white leather couch before he even tried folding up his long legs to sit on the hearthrug.

'If you think I'm going to be responsible for pizza stains on Marsh's precious white couch, you're foolish,' Torey announced.

'Who's complaining?' Stan said bravely. 'As picnics go, I guess this is more my style than a blanket in the woods.' He held out his hands to the blaze.

'And the only aunt we have to watch out for here is Violet.' Torey sank her teeth into the first slice of pepperoni and sausage and cheese, and gave a contented sigh.

'That sounds like a leading remark.'

'Oh, the pipes have been rattling a lot today. I suppose it's only air in them from all the work Gus has been doing, but still...' And the rest of it, she told herself, is a combination of too much time to think and a still guilty conscience over what had happened last night. As if Violet could know or care what I think of Marsh Endicott...

'That's a bit ghostly.' Stan looked around. 'I know how Marsh gets on your nerves, but I'm awfully glad you're not living here alone, Torey. This big old house—don't you ever dream of a tiny, snug little apartment?'

She shook her head. 'Never. I dream of the money to do something wonderful with this place—and the freedom not to have to consult Marsh.'

'And Kimberley,' Stan murmured.

'Her, too. Where did he find her, anyway? In a block of ice at the North Pole?' She lay back on the hearthrug and stared through half-closed eyes at the carved mouldings at ceiling level. 'She must have left right after we did.'

'So I could have come in last night after all?'

Torey felt her face flame and turned quickly towards the fire to conceal the tell-tale flush.

'This is getting to be a serious grudge.' Stan sounded a bit absent-minded. He leaned over her. 'You've got cheese smeared on your chin. Let me get it.'

He kissed it off, and then casually turned his attention to her mouth. She relaxed and let him hold her, almost willing herself to feel the same sort of firestorm that had swept through her last night in this room. But Stan's kiss, while pleasant and nice and a bit tingly, just didn't have the same electricity.

Forbidden fruit, she told herself, always tastes the sweetest, for a while at least. But remember well, Torey—it rots first, too.

Marsh was still drinking coffee on Monday morning when Torey came downstairs. She hadn't expected him to be there, and his mere silent presence sent shivers chasing each other in waves over her whole body. It didn't help that she was still wearing her terry bathrobe, and that he gave her attire a jaundiced look. She put two slices of wheat bread in Violet's old toaster and poured herself a glass of orange juice that she didn't want. 'Is Gus off on another job?' she asked.

'No, he'll be here. Why?'

She gestured with her glass at his neatly knotted tie and the heather-tweed sports jacket draped over the back of the chair. 'Because you've obviously given up the life of a plumber's helper.'

'I thought I'd better get back to making the money to pay him. Besides, he doesn't need a helper for a while.'

'That's good. I thought you might have apprenticed me.'

He didn't smile. Obviously, Torey thought, he had left his sense of humour somewhere over the weekend.

Her toast emerged, pale tan and still doughy in the middle, black around the edges. Torey sighed and carried it over to the sink to scrape off the areas that had turned to carbon. 'I'm really sorry about what happened Saturday night,' she said, over her shoulder. 'It certainly didn't do anything for my self-esteem, and it obviously stung your pride, as well.'

'Don't worry about my pride. I haven't got any to speak of.'

'That's not the impression I——'

'If it comes to a choice between keeping my dignity or fighting for what I want, I'll fight, no matter how silly I might end up looking.'

The brusqueness of the statement nearly floored her. 'Well, don't worry about your dignity,' she snapped. 'I'm certainly not so proud of what happened that I'd go around bragging about it!'

'That's a relief.' He pushed his chair back and dumped the dregs of his coffee down the drain. 'Kimberley is planning to stop by this morning.'

Torey stopped smearing jam on her toast. 'What happened to the idea of letting me concentrate on my work?

Take 4 Medical Romances

Mills & Boon Medical Romances capture the excitement, intrigue and emotion of the busy medical world. A world often interrupted by love and romance...

We will send you 4 BRAND NEW MEDICAL ROMANCES absolutely FREE plus a cuddly teddy bear and a surprise mystery gift, as your introduction to this superb series.

At the same time we'll reserve a subscription for you to our Reader

Service. Every two months you could receive the 6 latest Medical Romances delivered direct to your door POST AND PACKING FREE, plus a free Newsletter packed with competitions, author news and much, much more.

What's more there's no obligation, you can cancel or suspend your subscription at any time. So you've nothing to lose and a whole world of romance to gain!

FREE

Your Free Gifts!

We'll send you this cute little tan and white teddy bear plus a surprise gift when you return this card. So don't delay.

If you think that allowing that frigid female to have the run of this house is going to get me out of here...'

He scratched his chin as if he was giving serious thought, not to what she had said, but to the reasons behind it.

Torey smothered a sigh. Saying catty things about Kimberley only guarantees that you'll see more of her, she told herself. When will you learn, Farrell?

But all he said was, 'She wants to look the house over again.'

'With an eye to redecorating, I suppose?' Torey asked sweetly. 'Didn't she succeed in changing your mind about building? I was certain she'd be very persuasive——'

He cut briskly across the interruption. 'Sorry to disappoint you, Torey, but I haven't given up on the house.'

Torey considered it. 'I'm still placing my bets on Kimberley. How much are you offering for my half now, by the way?'

He shook his head. 'No offer. The time-limit expired, so now it's up to you.'

'I set my price, and we negotiate? I suppose that's intended to make me feel threatened so I'll set it low?'

'I don't see any reason to discuss my strategy with you.'

'I'll think it over. By the way, which half of the house is Kimberley planning to decorate? I hope she hasn't set her heart on the kitchen. I'm growing rather fond of this colour.'

He rubbed his temples as if he was feeling a little ill. 'You don't have to follow her around and take notes, you know.'

She asked, with deceptive sweetness, 'Will it be adequate if I retire to the attic?'

'Victoria, don't be such a——' He stopped. 'Just let her in, all right? And stay out of the way.' He pulled the heather-tweed sports jacket on with a violence that threatened its well-tailored seams, grabbed his down coat and went out the back door carrying it, in too much of a hurry to bother with putting it on.

It was barely half an hour later, and Gus the plumber was only starting work, when the doorbell rang.

Torey swore at the interruption—her cartoon was just coming together—and went to answer it. So much for working today, she muttered. Because, no matter what orders Marsh had tried to issue, she had no intention of turning Kimberley Cameron loose in the house. It was still half Torey's, after all.

It was not Kimberley on the veranda, but Marsh's mother instead, in a red wool coat with the collar turned up against the wind.

'Mrs Endicott,' Torey stammered. 'Marsh has already left for work, I'm afraid——'

'I know. I saw all I wanted to see of Marsh yesterday.'

He was with his mother yesterday, she thought blankly. Not with Kimberley after all. Then she reminded herself that the two were not mutually exclusive. It had probably been a warm little family party.

'I came to talk to you, Miss Farrell.'

There seemed to be a sudden nervous tic in the middle of Torey's throat, like a hiccup that had stuck. She swallowed hard, but it didn't help. 'I'm afraid I——'

Dolores Endicott smiled; it was like the sun breaking slowly through the clouds of a grey winter day. Marsh had inherited his father's eyes, Torey found herself thinking, but he had his mother's smile . . . And why was the woman smiling at her, when the next move would surely be to try to persuade her to let Marsh have his wish? Or was she on Kimberley's side of this squabble?

Torey shook her head just a little, to try to clear it. The thing was getting too complicated for her, that was certain.

'It will only take a moment,' Dolores went on. 'The president of The Players said you'd agreed to help with the advertising brochure for the next production, and I thought we could make a date to work on it.'

Torey started to breathe again. 'Of course,' she said weakly. 'But——' She stopped dead, a little afraid of what might come out next if she didn't control her tongue.

'It will have to be soon, I'm afraid. Marsh has told me how busy you are, but the printing deadlines are creeping up.' And then Dolores Endicott smiled again, apologetically this time, but with the same effect, and Torey found herself stepping back from the door and inviting the woman in.

That was how it happened that, when Kimberley rang the doorbell an hour later, Torey didn't move from the couch. She simply took her pencil from between her teeth, called, 'Come in!' and pulled a page out of the stack of mock-ups that were spread out on the coffee-table in front of them. 'Dolores, how about using this for the cover—a more polished version of it, of course— and then repeating the motif throughout the booklet in silhouettes? They'll be bold and striking, but fast and simple to do—Oh, hello, Kimberley. I'm a bit busy this morning, but Marsh already gave you the tour, didn't he?'

Kimberley turned slightly purple.

Dolores Endicott offered her cheek for Kimberley to kiss; the young woman's red-painted lips obediently brushed the air beside it. 'Hello, Kimberley, dear,' Dolores murmured. 'Torey, that's a brilliant notion. Marsh told me you were talented——'

'Mother Endicott,' Kimberley said firmly. 'You've met Sterling Granville, haven't you? I'm sure you've seen his work.'

The tall, blond young man beside her stopped eyeing the carved mouldings at ceiling-level and bowed gracefully from the waist. His jacket was cut to give the effect of a cape; it, more than Kimberley's introduction, screamed his profession. 'I am charmed,' he said, with only a hint of a French accent. Torey wondered if it was real.

Dolores obediently offered her hand. 'Mr Granville, of course I've seen your work. The rooms you design are—unique.'

Kimberley beamed. 'We are so fortunate to have him here in Springhill, aren't we? Sterling is going to give me some ideas of what might be done to salvage this house.'

The young man said, 'This room is unbelievable.'

Kimberley made a face. 'Yes, isn't it? And wait till you see what's upstairs—some really incredible hand-designed wallpaper, among other things.' She sent a catty smile towards Torey.

Sterling obviously wasn't listening. 'The proportions—the light . . .' He said, suddenly, 'Silver. I see your drawing-room in silver. Watered silk on the walls, a pale, muted area carpet. We'll tint the floor to pale grey, and the woodwork, too.' He looked up at the chandeliers again as if for inspiration, and said, 'Those must go, of course. We'll cloud the ceiling, and put a hand-loomed tapestry on that thing.'

For an instant Torey thought he meant her, then she realised he was merely pointing an accusing finger at the couch she was sitting on.

'If you insist on keeping it,' he went on, with a grudging note. 'I'd recommend you don't.'

'It belongs to Marsh,' Kimberley said.

'Ah, then . . .' He dismissed it with a wave of his hand. 'I suppose we could bear to put it in his den. This room should be very French—very *you*.' He raised Kimberley's hand to his lips with a triumphant air. She looked at him adoringly and without a word led him into the dining-room.

'Just make yourselves at home,' Torey called after them. There was no answer.

She kept her silence till she heard the Gallic shriek that meant Sterling Granville had just encountered the lime-green kitchen. Then she said, thoughtfully, '"Cloud the ceiling?"'

Dolores didn't look up. 'He does it in at least one room of every house. It's become his trademark, I think, though lord knows anyone can spot a Sterling Granville decorating job, because they all look alike. He paints the ceiling blue and then speckles it with white blotches—it's supposed to look like the great outdoors on a summer afternoon.'

'I thought it must be something like that. And what about "tint the woodwork"? Does that mean what I think it does, too?'

'Peasants like you and me would say, we'll paint it,' Dolores agreed.

Torey took one comprehensive look at Dolores' winter-white suit and the string of pearls that nestled comfortably against the soft red blouse, and she decided that she didn't mind at all being in the company of this sort of peasant.

'But of course Sterling and his crowd never *paint* anything. It sounds too lower class.'

'The last time I looked,' Torey said carefully, 'this was still a Victorian house. And making a fake French drawing-room out of what is a simple, elegant parlour——'

'I know,' Dolores sighed. 'It smacks of making a sow's ear out of a silk purse, doesn't it? But if that's what Marsh wants...'

There was no doubt in Torey's mind that she was not talking about Sterling Granville and a silver drawing-room.

Dolores smiled with determination. 'I don't often slip up like that,' she said. 'I beg your pardon, Torey. Now, if we've decided on the cover...'

With the kitchen inspection obviously finished, Kimberley practically danced up the stairs with Sterling Granville following. He stopped every step or two to study some detail, but he had ceased talking altogether, as far as Torey could see. She wondered if he was in a creative mist, or just shocked at the extent of destruction he was going to have to cause to please Kimberley. He obviously knew the kind of thing she liked—a French drawing-room, indeed! Surely if the man had any credentials—or any common sense—at all, he could see what he was doing, Torey thought. Didn't he care anything for the beauty he was destroying, the simple grace of the old house that would have to give way to make room for Kimberley's cosmetically applied elegance? And as for Marsh—he had apparently already given Kimberley permission to do whatever she liked, in return for her agreeing to live here at all.

Kimberley and Sterling came rattling back down the stairs. 'That awful tub,' Kimberley was saying. 'I don't even like to look at it. I'd never be convinced it was clean. We'll have to put a whirlpool in the master bathroom, of course.'

'Heart-shaped pink marble,' Sterling agreed, with explanatory gestures.

Torey wanted to stand up and scream, 'Doesn't anybody but me care about this house?' If at that moment Marsh had renewed his offer to buy her half, she might have taken him up on it, just so she didn't have to listen to any more of Kimberley's cock-eyed ideas. How, she wondered, had the woman managed to travel Europe without absorbing a single fragment of good taste?

Marsh was getting what he deserved, she thought, but even Marsh's stubbornness couldn't keep him blinded forever. Still, by the time he woke up, this incredible pair would have finished destroying the house.

Well, there wasn't much she could do to stop it, but she would stick it out as long as she could, for Violet's sake, she decided.

That was when she first realised that she had given up on having the house for herself, that she had surrendered to the certainty that someday, inevitably, Marsh would have it, because there were forces here that she could not fight. Money was the least of them. Standing by and watching as the house was destroyed—well, that was something else.

She wondered suddenly if Marsh knew that too, and if he had planned it that way.

'How soon can you have the whole decorating scheme put together?' Kimberley was asking eagerly, at the front door.

'Dear lady, for you, I'll do it as soon as I can. Not all the finished plans and drawings, perhaps, but quick sketches, samples, swatches of fabrics—all ready to show to your Marsh.'

'What a darling you are, Sterling...' Kimberley's voice faded, and the front door banged. Torey could understand how Kimberley could forget all about her, but surely even in her ecstatic condition the girl should have remembered to show respect for her future mother-in-law by saying goodbye.

'You know,' Dolores said thoughtfully, 'the way this living-room looks, I'm afraid even grey watered silk would look like an improvement.'

Torey nodded. 'This paper must be thirty years old.'

'At least.' Dolores walked across the room and without regard for a perfectly manicured fingernail picked a corner loose near the fireplace. 'Look what's underneath. Roses. I'd forgotten all about Ward's mother's roses.'

Torey came across to look. They were delicate red roses, climbing and weaving around trellises. 'Beautiful,' she said. 'But I'd put up spring wild flowers instead—like a subtle woodland garden.'

'Why don't you?' Dolores asked softly.

Torey scratched her head with the eraser end of her pencil. 'You mean, beat Kimberley to the punch? Redecorate before she has a chance to?'

For the briefest of moments, Torey could see the completed room, the soft pastel flowers on the walls, the furniture polished to a gleam, the friends gathered in this gentle, inviting atmosphere. And then she remembered the painful realisation of a few minutes ago, that this could never truly be her house, that Marsh would inevitably win, and Kimberley would have her heart's wish.

'I couldn't,' she said.

Dolores mused, 'I used to hang wallpaper. And it's like riding a bike—you never forget how.'

'Well, I never have.' But Torey was wavering a little. You need to get back to your own work, part of her brain was arguing. You can't win, so you should give in with dignity. Don't make a fool of yourself.

It reminded her of what Marsh had said just this morning: 'If it comes to a choice between keeping my dignity or fighting for what I want, I'll fight, no matter how silly I might end up looking.'

That's different, she told herself. There's no question, really, of fighting for the house now.

'I don't have that kind of cash lying around,' she said.

There was a twinkle in Dolores' eyes. 'Oh, I think if you're going to do the work it would only be fair if Marsh supplied the paper.'

'I wouldn't dare charge it to him,' Torey said, but her voice quavered a little.

'I would. But perhaps it would be better if I made him a gift of it. What about it, Torey?'

It would be so much more pleasant, if she was going to live here for even a few more weeks...

Oh, at least be honest, Torey, she ordered herself. You could continue to live with the wallpaper as it is. The truth is, you just want to see Kimberley's face. You want to make her work for it. At least that way she'll have to look at what she's destroying.

She took hold of the tiny corner that Dolores had pulled loose and tugged. The wallpaper yielded with a satisfying rip, coming away from the plaster in a great swath.

Dolores rubbed her hands together and said with a smile, 'This is going to be a snap.'

CHAPTER SEVEN

IT WAS not a snap; by mid-afternoon, Torey was beginning to wonder why she had let herself be talked into the project at all. Her wrist was aching from the unaccustomed, repetitive scraping. She was standing in a pile of wet and bedraggled scraps of old wallpaper, her shoes covered with the sticky residue of the glue she was scraping from the plaster, and every time she moved she rustled. She walked over to Marsh's white leather couch, now draped with heavy plastic, and flopped down on it with a sigh.

'Why is it,' she asked, 'that a mere two layers of wallpaper can make a pile on the floor that's three feet deep?'

From her perch high on a ladder at the other end of the room, Dolores grinned, not taking her eyes from the strip of new paper she was patiently smoothing against the wall. 'Be grateful it isn't seven layers—Violet at least did that much right.' She gave a last brush to the strip and leaned back to take good a look, then climbed down a couple of steps and began to work again. 'We're a lot further along than it looks.'

Torey looked at the three big black plastic bags already stuffed to bursting with debris, and the one wall that was beginning to look like a woodland flower garden. She studied her hands, wrinkled from long immersion in water, and noted that she was covered with discoloured old paste all the way to the elbows. She glanced at Dolores, who looked as fresh as one of the wallpaper flowers in her Chinese blue jogging-suit, even after hours atop the ladder, and wondered idly if the woman had taken off her pearls when she'd gone home to change clothes, or if she was still wearing them underneath the high-necked jacket.

Then Torey sighed and hauled herself up from the couch and went back to work, smearing hot water on the old paper, patiently waiting for it to soak in, mechanically scraping it off.

The high point of the afternoon was when she found the names of the original paper-hangers scrawled in pencil on the plaster by the dining-room doorway. Dolores even came down off her ladder to see that, and they solemnly added their names as well.

They were working on the long fireplace wall, trying to get the paper smoothed just so around the carved end of the mantel, when Marsh said, from the dining-room door, 'What in the hell do you think you're doing?'

Neither of them had heard him come in. Torey whirled around, guilt written in every line of her face as she saw, not only Marsh in the doorway, but Kimberley beside him. 'Now we're in for it,' she muttered.

Even Dolores seemed to be taken aback; she had just started down the ladder, and she missed a rung and had to grab at the mantel for support. Then she sat down on the bottom step with one foot extended, folded her arms, and said, calmly, 'Well, you caught us, Marsh. Hello again, Kimberley.'

Marsh dropped an armful of sample books carelessly on the couch's plastic cover and turned on Kimberley. 'I thought you had enough sense not to start working the place over just yet——'

'Me?' she retorted. 'You can't think that I had anything to do with this! It was *her*!' She pointed a dramatic finger at Torey, who would have crawled into the fireplace and up the chimney if Dolores' ladder hadn't been in the way.

She bit her lip and succeeded only in looking guiltier. Marsh studied her for a long moment, then slowly shook his head, as if he couldn't quite believe what he was seeing. 'I should have known,' he muttered.

'Mother Endicott,' Kimberley said stiffly, 'how could you allow this—person—to influence you into doing this?'

'Nothing influenced me, Kimberley dear, except the wish to do something thoughtful for my son. I was having so much trouble thinking of something just right for your birthday present, darling.' Dolores blew Marsh an elaborate kiss. 'And then this just popped into my head.'

Kimberley stalked across the room. 'But this is nothing like what I intended to do with this room! It will all have to be ripped off before my silver watered silk can go up. I don't know what Sterling will say——'

'Why does it have to go?' Marsh asked suddenly. 'I kind of like the flowers.'

Kimberley's face seemed to puff up slightly, and her olive skin turned an unpleasant shade of red. 'I refuse to dignify that with a comment,' she said stiffly. 'If you don't have enough sense to know the difference between a decorator's vision and this—this amateurish non-sense——'

Marsh pushed his sports jacket back and hooked his thumbs in his trouser pockets. 'I have enough sense to know what I like,' he said calmly. 'And I'm not much on a dingy grey living-room. Your fancy new colour scheme sounded pretty much like what it already was—dull.'

Torey blinked in surprise.

'Not living-room. Drawing-room,' Kimberley said between her teeth. 'Not grey—silver. And no Sterling Granville design could ever be dull.'

'That's the truth,' Torey muttered. 'Cloudy ceilings and tinted woodwork and all.'

Kimberley shot her a look that should have turned her to a cinder. 'Do you suppose we could have this discussion without an audience, Marshall?'

He shrugged. 'Personally, I think the ladies have a stake in the matter.'

'Very well,' Kimberley said. 'If you insist on embarrassing yourself in front of your mother and your—companion—who am I to argue?'

'Embarrassing myself?' He shook his head. 'I don't think that's quite what you mean, Kimberley, so you might as well say what you're thinking.'

'Very well, Marsh, I will.' She stamped her small foot. 'I think it is time you knew that I am sick of your selfish demands. You didn't even consult me about this house—you simply moved into it and announced that we would live here. You absolutely refuse to listen to what I want. Very well—I've given in to your petty tyranny and agreed. I'll live here, if you insist on occupying these four walls. But the inside of my house is my concern, and if I want a silver drawing-room I am going to have it! It's the least you can do. If you would only consider everything I'm giving up for you——'

'I have,' Marsh said. 'And you can add the silver drawing-room to the list. It doesn't belong in this house.'

'Sterling is a genius, Marsh. How can you possibly turn your back on his vision, when he went to such trouble——?'

Marsh expressed an opposing opinion of Sterling Granville's worth in one brief, idiomatic and extremely rude sentence. From the look on Dolores' face, Torey concluded that Marsh's mother had never heard him use those words before.

Kimberley smiled, but it looked as if it hurt her. 'All right,' she went on patiently. 'If you are so very opposed to doing the necessary work to bring this house up to a liveable in condition, then there is only one sensible compromise.'

'I'd like to hear what it is,' Torey said under her breath.

'There's a house out on the north edge of town that is almost completed. Sterling has already looked at it, and he says it can be easily adapted to everything I want——'

'That's a compromise?' Marsh asked.

'Oh, do be reasonable, Marsh. It's the perfect solution.'

He didn't answer.

Kimberley took it as agreement. 'Then I'll call him tomorrow, and we can go and look at——'

'No, Kimberley. I'm not giving up my house.' Oddly enough, it sounded almost gentle.

Kimberley stared at him for a long moment. 'I suppose the next thing you'll refuse to give up is the blonde tomato.' She jerked a hand towards Torey.

Dolores pursed her lips as if she'd unexpectedly bitten into something sour. 'Tomato?' she said indistinctly.

Marsh glanced at his mother with a faint smile. 'I can't exactly throw her out,' he began. 'I've told you before, Kimberley, she——'

'All right, Marsh, that's it,' Kimberley said harshly. 'I've had it. Obviously you don't give a damn about me, or what would make me happy. Well, I'm no longer so blind that I think you'll change. The whole thing was a mistake, and I'm calling it off—understood?'

She tugged the diamond ring off her left hand with a fierce yank and threw it at him. It struck the knot of his necktie and bounced into the bucket of wallpaper paste. It was impossible, Torey told herself, that the splash it made actually echoed through the room. It was only her imagination.

Nevertheless, it was very silent in the living-room; the only sound was the click of Kimberley's footsteps and the whispery murmur of the long strip of discarded wallpaper that had stuck to her shoe. She paused in the hallway to rip it off her sole, and she slammed the front door so hard that the bevelled glass in the living-room windows shivered.

'The Players,' Dolores said thoughtfully. She still hadn't moved from her perch on the lowest step of the ladder. 'That kind of talent is always in demand. We'll have to recruit her for The Players.'

Marsh walked across the room to stand in front of Dolores, his hands on his hips. 'Mother,' he said, looking down at her with an expression Torey couldn't quite place. Was it irritation? Frustration? Simple confusion? 'I never thought I would see the day when you would take part in anything of this sort.'

'That's wonderful, darling,' Dolores said briskly. 'I'm glad you respect me so much.'

'That wasn't quite what I——'

Dolores interrupted the protest. 'Now will you take me over to the hospital, Marsh?' She shifted her position a little, and winced in pain. 'I think I broke my ankle when I slipped off the ladder.'

Torey was on her hands and knees on the living-room floor, trying to remove the last traces of old wallpaper and paste from the hardwood, when Marsh came back a couple of hours later.

'What are you doing?' he asked.

'Penance.' She didn't even look up as she asked, warily, 'Is it broken?'

'No, just badly sprained. It will give her a good excuse to sit still and eat chocolates for a few days.'

'That's a relief,' Torey muttered. 'I could just see her in a cast up to here.'

'Whatever inspired you to drag my mother into this scheme, anyway, Torey?'

She pushed her bucket aside and sat down cross-legged on the floor with a bang. 'Drag your mother?' she asked, her voice rising. 'I didn't! For your information, Marsh, your mother is dangerous.'

'Oh, come on! You expect me to believe that she came barging in here with rolls of wallpaper in her arms, saying, "Let's see how much trouble we can cause with Kimberley"?'

'Very nearly.' Torey realised that she was sitting too near a puddle for continued comfort, and started to scrub again. 'And speaking of the great lady, why are you here? Or have you and Kimberley already patched it up? Did you agree to look at her new house, or have you decided to try to evict me instead?'

'Evict you?' he said mildly. 'Get rid of the blonde tomato? Then what would I do for entertainment?'

She looked suspiciously over her shoulder at him and saw that he was giving her another of those long, appraising looks. From that angle, she realised, her sweat-suit probably didn't look baggy at all. She grew three shades pinker and quickly turned around to face him. 'Well, whenever you decide to make up with her,' she said a little breathlessly, 'I recommend a bit of hand-kissing. It seemed to do wonders for Sterling Granville this morning.'

She pushed herself up from the floor—the work wasn't finished, but she was darned if she'd stay there and encourage him to watch—and carried her bucket to the kitchen to dump it. She scrubbed her hands meticulously, mourned the demise of the ten perfectly good fingernails she had possessed that morning, and wearily opened the refrigerator door to investigate its contents. The left-over tuna casserole was not exactly inspiring, but right now she wasn't in the mood to create anything else.

Marsh had followed her. 'The least you can do after all the trouble you've caused,' he said, 'is take a shower and go out to dinner with me.'

She shook her head a little to clear it and took the casserole dish out. 'I don't think I'm hearing quite right. What on earth are you celebrating? Is it honestly your birthday?'

'Your heard it on the best of authority. Don't you think my mother should know?'

'I thought it was a convenient fiction.'

'And since she is in no condition to cook my favourite meal, thanks to your cock-eyed schemes——'

'Not altogether mine,' Torey defended.

He grinned at her. 'Good—at least you're now admitting that you were involved.' Before she could open her mouth to protest, he went on, 'And since Kimberley isn't speaking to me, also thanks to you——'

'That reminds me. I thought this was the best thing to do with it.' Torey reached into a cupboard and handed him a tumbler full of cloudy water. At the bottom rested a diamond ring, its sparkle hidden by the residue of wallpaper paste that continued to cling stubbornly to it. 'It'll have to go back to the jeweller right away.' Then she realised that there was more than one interpretation to what she had said, and she added quickly, 'To be cleaned, I mean.'

'Of course,' Marsh said gently. 'What on earth else would you have meant? What about it, Torey? Are you going to dinner with me?'

She knew he was using her; he was capable of anything, and he'd certainly had time to think the whole thing over and plan his attack. The news that he had taken Torey out to dinner on the very night his engagement was broken would certainly fly back to

Kimberley's ears, and if she was already regretting what she had done this afternoon...

No wonder he hadn't gone straight back to the woman tonight, Torey thought; that would have meant his unconditional surrender, and Marsh would never do that. He was going to lay a slow siege instead, and Torey herself was his chosen weapon.

If you get involved you're a damned fool, she told herself. Then she looked at the tuna casserole again and thought longingly of prime rib with rare juices and lobster with drawn butter and veal with cream sauce, and made up her mind.

'Look,' she said bluntly, 'I know what you're doing, and I don't approve.'

He looked down at the floor, as if a bit ashamed of himself. Under the glare of the ceiling light, his eyelashes made a heavy, dark shadow against his high cheekbones.

Torey was proud of herself. So he hadn't expected her to see through that, had he? 'On the other hand, it's none of my business what strategy you use to convince Kimberley that she should come crawling back to you.'

His gaze lifted to meet hers steadily, and his voice was calm. 'You're right,' he mused. 'It isn't.'

It should have made her feel better, but it didn't. She ruthlessly suppressed the uncomfortable feeling.

'Besides,' he went on, 'you owe me a little co-operation. You're the cause of it all.'

'I do not for one minute admit that I'm responsible for your broken engagement. But I'll go along with your little scheme, on one condition.'

'And that is?' He sounded suspicious.

She fluttered her eyelashes at him and did her best to make her voice sound sultry and seductive. 'Is there any place in town that has decent seafood? I'm dying for a huge plate of scallops.'

His eyes narrowed, and for an instant she thought she'd overdone the acting. Then he gave a great shout of laughter, put one arm around her waist, lifted her off her feet and swung her around the kitchen. 'Co-operate with me, Victoria,' he promised, 'and you shall have all the scallops you can eat!'

He took her to the country club. Even on a Monday night, the place was busy. The lounge was thronged with men watching a basketball game and the lobby was full of women coming and going from committee meetings. The dining-room was quieter, and they got the intimate little corner table that Marsh requested, but there were enough people scattered around throughout the large room to be assured that the gossip would fly.

Which, she told herself, was exactly what he intended to happen.

He waved the waiter away and held Torey's chair with an elegant flourish, then let his hands rest on her shoulders for the briefest of moments before taking his own seat beside her. It sent a delightful little chill through her.

Don't forget, Torey Farrell, she reminded herself, that you're only substitute material here. It would be all too easy to get used to this kind of treatment...

So, just to reinforce that knowledge, she congratulated Marsh on his choice. 'Kimberley's probably already heard about it,' she said, closing her menu and laying it aside.

'I wouldn't doubt it.' He didn't sound concerned.

Of course he wasn't worried, Torey thought. He must know to a nicety just how stubborn Kimberley Cameron was and how long her resistance was likely to last. He wasn't going to get impatient. And that, she reminded herself, is absolutely none of your concern. You're being well-paid, in scallops.

He gave their order to the waiter and sat back, his elbows propped on the arms of his chair, watching her thoughtfully.

'Having second thoughts?' he asked.

'Yes, as a matter of fact. If you believe that taking me out for dinner once will make Kimberley come whimpering back to you, I think you're sadly mistaken.'

'Why, Torey, I didn't think you'd descend to hinting,' he said promptly.

Torey's head was reeling a bit. 'Hinting? That we should make a habit of this? I certainly didn't——' She stopped abruptly, just as the waiter arrived with a silver bucket and a bottle of wine. Marsh approved the wine and filled her glass. She sipped it a little nervously.

'It wasn't fair of me to accuse you of hinting, was it?' Marsh asked.

'It certainly wasn't,' Torey said, a little grumpily.

'Because I agree completely. It will probably take a week at least.' Marsh reached for a bread stick, snapped it in half, and handed her a piece. 'Don't worry about it—I promised you all the scallops you can eat, and I'm a man of my word.'

It took a bit to get her breath back. She sipped her wine slowly. To all appearances she was savouring the bouquet; in actual fact it was a delaying tactic. 'That's not quite what I agreed to, you know,' she said finally, and was proud of her restraint. 'And I do have other plans.'

'You mean Stan? You're not really serious about him, are you?'

'That's beside the point.'

'That means you aren't,' he said comfortably.

'It doesn't matter if I am or not. I'm not about to tell him to get lost, just to support this incredible scheme of yours!'

Marsh swirled the wine in his glass and smiled. 'You don't have to get rid of him.'

'Well, I'm glad to have your permission to keep seeing him!' she said with sweet cynicism. 'After all, it's nothing to me whether or not you and Kimberley patch it up.'

It didn't seem to bother him. 'That's right; you said yourself that it's none of your business. So why shouldn't you spend a little time with me? Let me worry about the implications. You just think about the scallops.'

The waiter brought their soup, a delicately spicy concoction of herbs and mushrooms and cream, and she fell silent while she sampled it.

'Of course,' Marsh said thoughtfully, 'if you would like to put Stan on hold for a week or so——'

'I wouldn't,' she said crisply. 'I suppose the next thing you're going to explain to me—in the fond belief that I'm going to go along with this—is the ground rules for this scam of yours. All right, I'll listen politely. Am I dressed properly? And how, precisely, should a tomato behave?' She leaned forward and placed a small hand on his sleeve. The muscle under the tweed felt hard and warm.

'I could give you a few suggestions,' he suggested drily, 'but I don't think you need to hear them.'

She drew back abruptly, and sat up straight. 'If you think that I make a habit of this——'

A gleam of humour sprang to life in Marsh's eyes. 'I just meant that I don't think you have to try,' he murmured. He reached for her hand. 'Just acting your normal self has already been enough to get Kimberley's goat.'

'I told you a long time ago it would be,' she said, trying to ignore the fact that his fingers were now interlaced with hers, and their hands lay on the corner of the table.

'Yes,' Marsh said thoughtfully. 'I believe the last time you mentioned it was Saturday night, by the fire...'

Torey could feel the embarrassed heat start in her toes and flood upwards until she was burning with it.

Marsh smiled and let her hand slip out of his, and picked up his spoon again. To someone watching from across the room, it must have looked like the slow and reluctant relinquishing of a lover, she thought. Well, that's what you get for issuing a challenge like that, Farrell.

'Isn't there anyone else you could ask to do this, Marsh? Old girlfriends?'

'Can't think of a one.'

Torey's voice was dry. 'You expect me to believe that you've had no other girlfriends?'

His smile flashed. 'I didn't say that. I meant, I couldn't think of any who wouldn't take me seriously if I came around again.'

'Well, I'm guaranteed not to do that.'

'Besides, Kimberley herself gave you the perfect build-up.'

'The blonde tomato. Don't remind me. How long have you and Kimberley been dating, anyway?'

Marsh shrugged. 'A few years.'

She choked on her soup. 'A few *years*?' she sputtered. 'No wonder you were willing to wait till after her busy season to get married. It must have been hardly any sacrifice at all.'

There was a gleam in his eyes. 'You don't believe in long engagements?' he asked blandly.

Torey bit her tongue. 'I'm sorry. That just slipped out, Marsh.'

'Truth often does. What about taking time to get to know one another? Or don't you believe in that, either?'

'Of course. But I don't think it generally takes years. Tell the truth, Marsh, haven't you been getting a little impatient? And don't you have any doubts? I mean, I saw the way she kissed you that day——'

'Ah. You're a peeping Torey, too.'

She coloured a little. 'Believe me, it was no big thrill! If that's the best she can do for a kiss——'

It was fortunate that the waiter returned just then to retrieve their soup plates. It gave Torey a moment to reconsider.

'You were saying?' Marsh prompted.

'I think I've said enough already. Sorry—my tongue runs away with me sometimes. I'll bet *that* never happens to Kimberley, either.'

He looked thoughtful. 'Then you think she really meant it this afternoon?'

'Of course she did. Whether she still means it tonight is the real question you should be asking yourself.' She sipped her wine and added, thoughtfully, 'I'm betting it costs you the new house.'

He was watching her intently. 'And if it does? What would you do if I moved out?'

Torey shrugged and smiled. 'Pay you a reasonable rent, of course.'

'You seriously intend to stay in Springhill?'

'Why not? Lots of people obviously like it here—why not me?'

He sounded dissatisfied. 'There's really nobody waiting for you in California?'

'Swarms of men,' Torey said promptly 'That's mainly what I'm escaping from. There was just no peace anywhere I went.'

He smothered a smile. 'Well, you're not likely to have that problem here.'

'That's certainly not a polite thing to say to—oh, I see. You mean there just aren't many eligible men around.' She paused while the waiter placed her plate of scallops before her. 'That might change the picture,' she mused as she picked up her fork. 'Kimberley certainly knows that, and there's obviously no doubt in her mind about how eligible you are. So perhaps you won't have to buy the new house after all. But the silver drawing-room...' She shook her head. 'I'm afraid I don't see any way out of that at all. And it's such a pity.'

'After all your hard work,' he agreed.

'Well, of course, I won't——' She stopped abruptly.

There was an instant of silence, and then Marsh said, quietly, 'You won't—what? Be there to see the results?'

'You're still wishing for me to go away,' she said. Her voice was light-hearted, but it was an effort to keep it that way. 'Bad luck for you, Marsh.'

He didn't comment; instead he said, 'You know, you asked me the other day what Violet was like, and I didn't have much of an answer for you. I've been thinking about it lately, and I keep remembering one incident. It's funny, I hadn't thought of it in years.'

Torey put her fork down.

'I must have been about five,' Marsh said, 'and it was an afternoon—at least, I remember the sunshine streaming in the windows on the landing and making rainbows on the carpet.'

She nodded; she'd watched that effect herself. It didn't surprise her that a child would have remembered it.

'I'd found a cardboard box somewhere, and I was pretending that it was my sled and the stairs were a hill of snow. I must have made a fierce amount of noise sliding down. Violet caught me at the bottom and smacked me.'

'I'd have spanked you myself for that trick,' Torey murmured. 'That's a long flight. If you'd tipped the thing over——'

'For damaging the stairs.'

Torey blinked at him. 'You're joking,' she managed to say.

'No—and it's true, I'd scratched the finish. After that, when we went to visit, I had to sit in a chair. We didn't go often, thank heaven.'

'No wonder you don't have fond memories of Violet.'

He smiled ruefully. 'It should have been a wonderful house for children,' he mused. 'I used to sit there on that hard chair and think about how nice it would be to play hide and seek in that house. We lived in a little duplex then with not even a spare cupboard, much less an attic for excitement on rainy days. Have you ever thought of how tall that house looks to a child?'

Not how *big*, she thought, but how *tall*. It was an interesting perspective.

'So that's why you want it so badly,' she said. 'To annoy Violet's ghost by filling it with children.'

He laughed. 'I hadn't thought of it quite that way—but I suppose so.'

'Obviously you haven't told Kimberley this, or she'd understand why another house just won't do.' Torey speared her last scallop and dipped it in the remains of the garlic butter.

'I couldn't very well discuss it with her,' Marsh pointed out. 'I didn't really know it myself till you started asking questions.'

'Thanks,' Torey said drily, 'but I'd just as soon not get the credit for this one. How many kids are you planning on, anyway?'

He frowned. 'Well, I was an only child, and obviously that didn't do it. Six should be enough, don't you think?'

Torey felt a little faint at the idea. 'I'd think that half a dozen miniatures of you sliding down the stairs in a train of cardboard boxes would clear out not only Violet's ghost but cleaning ladies and babysitters and possibly their mother as well,' she said frankly.

The frown cleared. 'Four, then.'

'Marsh, you're hopeless. If I were in Kimberley's shoes, I'd——'

And then images began to assault her from nowhere, visions that had no base in reality at all, but only in an overheated imagination, she told herself desperately. Images of four little boys—or possibly six, it was hard to tell because they moved so fast—playing cowboys and Indians on the lawn of the tall old house. Of them sliding down banisters and falling out of treehouses and building snowmen in the middle of the driveway and turning the attic into a pirate ship and hijacking the biscuit jar. Four little boys—or possibly six—the image of Marsh . . .

Their mother would live in terror every day of her life, Torey thought. She'd be grey-haired by the time they were in school—and she would be happy. Not so much because of the little boys, she admitted, but because of their father . . .

She darted a sideways glance at Marsh, and was not surprised at the sudden rush of longing that closed her throat and almost brought tears to her eyes. Until today, he had been unavailable; an engaged man, like a married one, was off limits, and so she had not allowed herself to ask what it was that she was really feeling. But now she knew. She had been so upset with him over that kiss, not because he had been violating his pledge to Kimberley, but because she wanted him for herself. Some time in the last two weeks Torey had stopped concentrating on the determined stubbornness of him, and she had begun to see the gentleness underneath.

He's not dangerous, Stan had told her once. But, in fact, he was far more threatening to her peace of mind than any amount of violence could be. She had fallen in love with him, and that was the most frightening thing of all.

For her love could make no difference whatsoever. Though Marsh might be officially unengaged at the moment, he was not truly free, not so long as he wanted his fiancée back.

And a man who saw Torey only as a means to that end would never, ever look at her in any other light.

CHAPTER EIGHT

THOSE were the facts; that was all there was to be said about it.

I wish, she thought, that I had never come to Springhill.

Never? a little voice at the back of her brain asked. Would you really wish never to have seen him—never even to know that he existed? Surely not, Torey Farrell——

'What are you saying?' Marsh prompted. 'If you were in Kimberley's shoes...'

Torey let the tip of her tongue flick along her upper lip; the contact was dry and almost painful, and it brought her back to reality. 'Well, for one thing, my feet would hurt,' she said, trying to sound flippant. 'They're at least three sizes bigger than hers, you see.'

Marsh gave her one of those slow, seductive smiles that started in his eyes and seemed never to end at all. She watched for a few brief moments, until the devastating impact of it reached her diaphragm and threatened to choke off her breath altogether. Then she forced her attention back to the wine glass in her hand, studying the pattern of carved lines in the crystal goblet as intently as if she were going to have to reproduce it with her own hands. If she didn't look at him, she reasoned, then she couldn't actually throw herself into his arms...

Marsh reached for the wine bottle in the silver bucket. It was empty, and he started to look around for the waiter.

'No,' Torey said, hurriedly. 'I've had enough.' And a bit more than enough, her conscience reminded. Her head was starting to ring, but whether that was caused by the wine or by the knowledge that had burst so suddenly upon her was open to question, she had to admit.

'Dessert?' he asked.

Torey shook her head.

'Good choice. The chef isn't much of a hand with them—too stingy with the ingredients, I think. If you're ready to go...'

I'm not, she wanted to say. I want to sit here with you forever.

But instead she nodded and gathered up her handbag and went out of the dining-room with her hand politely on his arm. He held her coat and turned the collar up around her throat and smiled down into her eyes—largely for the benefit of the two matrons who were also in the cloakroom, Torey told herself. Still, it was nice to be treated that way.

Be honest, she told herself. It's nice to have Marsh treat you that way. There have been other men who acted as if you were a china doll with so little intelligence that you had to be dressed, and you hated it. But with Marsh...

He tucked her into the front of his sports car, and instead of driving back through town took the highway that looped around Springhill. On this clear, crisp spring night the warm gold of the city lights below the highway echoed the cold white stars above.

Torey sighed. 'It's beautiful—I've never seen anything quite like it.'

Marsh sounded doubtful. 'Stars?'

'Of course I've seen stars! Just not like this, that's all.' And not with you, her heart added. 'Can we stop and just look for a minute?'

He glanced at the clock on the dashboard and, without a word, turned on to the next side-road. It wasn't paved, and, even though he drove slowly, the tyres kicked rocks up against the car. Torey winced every time one hit; it was such a beautiful car.

'We should have brought mine,' she said. 'It doesn't matter if it gets battered up. Marsh, stopping on the edge of the highway would have been fine——'

'The view is better from up here. It's called Sentinel Oak.'

He was right about the view. Just then the road turned and widened into a sort of overlook, with the town spread out like a patchwork quilt below them. The actual difference in elevation from hilltop to town was probably only a few hundred feet, but the scene was more as if they were looking down from a mountain ledge on to a toy village. The panorama was framed by the huge bare limbs of an ancient oak tree, and the stars peeked between the branches like glistening ornaments.

'The Sentinel Oak,' Torey murmured. 'Standing here for a hundred years.' She eyed the gnarled trunk. 'Or more.'

'Just watching everything that goes on,' Marsh agreed. He turned the engine off and leaned back in his seat, his hands still loosely on the steering-wheel. 'Look.'

Across the valley, a tiny sliver of brilliant gold pushed its way up from the horizon. They watched in silence as the full moon crept silently into the night sky, dimming the glow of the stars, casting long shadows down from the hills and from the Sentinel Oak. The town below looked even more like a toy, now, scattered across the moonlit hills.

Only when the moon was fully launched on its nightly journey did Torey relax. She leaned back with a sigh. 'And people actually think this state is flat and featureless.'

'Parts of it are. But the glaciers didn't get this far south in the last Ice Age, so this section was never levelled out and polished off. And then the river cutting through the valley added——' He paused, and asked, 'Private joke? Or can anybody share?'

Torey was startled. 'I don't quite——'

'You were smiling, that's all.' He added gently, 'You should do it more often.'

The confused pleasure that touched her heart made her say, 'Oh, it was nothing, really. Just that we're sitting here at what's obviously a favourite hang-out for lovers, and we're honestly watching the moon rise and talking about geography. Or would it be geology?'

'Who cares?'

'At any rate, it's got to be a twist that old oak tree hasn't seen very often.' Stop it, Torey, she told herself in horror. You sound as if you're practically begging him to kiss you! She forced herself to laugh a little. 'I'm not making any sense, I'm afraid. Thank you for bringing me up here. It's a beautiful view.'

'Yes, it is.'

She glanced at him, warily, and then stared straight ahead. 'You're not looking at the moon any more, Marsh.'

'There are views, and then there are views,' he said cryptically. 'Your profile, for instance, is very nice.' His fingers cupped her chin and turned her gently to face him. 'But I'd rather see—this.'

It was a gentle, tentative kiss, with none of the violent intensity that had flared between them that night by the fire. His mouth was soft and warm and mobile against hers, taking without demanding, and Torey sighed and relaxed against him as best she could in the little car, drinking in the pleasure of that kiss. When he raised his head, she let hers fall back against the head-rest and opened her eyes, intending to smile at him and say something flippant about how now they could go home and leave the Sentinel Oak tree happy...

But what she saw in his eyes stopped her. The moon's glow falling over the oak's massive branches threw stripes of light and darkness across the car, and even in the shadow she could see the hunger stirring in him.

And she was afraid—not of him, but of herself. For her, this was no simple flirtation. It was not just a pleasant way to idle away an evening.

'Marsh, no——' But it was an uncertain whisper.

'Why not?' The question tickled; his mouth was soft against the little hollow at the base of her throat. He nibbled at the tender flesh, working his way slowly up to her chin. Finally he raised his head and looked down at her, his eyebrows arching. 'You still haven't answered the question,' he murmured, and kissed the corner of her mouth. 'Why not?'

Why not? She groped for a reason, anything at all that might make sense. 'Because I ate garlic for dinner,' she said desperately.

He smiled, that soft, slow smile again. 'I know,' he whispered. 'It tastes good on you, Victoria...'

This kiss was different. It was still tender, but there was a certainty about him now that had not been there before. His tongue slipped softly between her lips, caressing, probing, tasting. His fingers were busy with the buttons of her coat, and, when the last one yielded, his hands slipped under the tweed and found the spot where sweater and skirt met. Without an instant's hesitation, he began to stroke the sensitive flesh in long, gentle caresses, until his fingertips reached the delicate lace that covered her breasts.

She moaned a little. Her insides were beginning to feel a bit like a warm, carbonated soft drink. And Marsh, she thought fuzzily, was slowly and deliberately shaking the bottle.

I should stop this, she told herself. I should stop...

Before it gets out of hand? the little voice at the back of her brain asked. Don't kid yourself, Torey Farrell; it's already out of hand.

And after all, she asked herself, what did she have to lose? Why shouldn't she enjoy holding him, kissing him, making love with him, if she chose? Was there anything so wrong with seizing the fleeting pleasure she could have? The evening had been a revelation to her; perhaps it had been a surprise to him as well. He had said himself that he and Kimberley had dated for years; if he had honestly loved her, could he have been so patient? And if he didn't truly care for Kimberley, then perhaps——

Don't count on it, she tried to tell herself. Don't count on anything.

But that undoubtedly wise counsel was not solid enough to withstand the desire growing within her, and so she tried to pull him down to her, to bring him even closer.

He grunted a little, as if in pain. Her eyes snapped open, instantly concerned. He smiled ruefully and rubbed his thigh where it had collided with the gear stick. 'Damn sports cars,' he muttered. 'I'm getting too old for this. You're right; we should have brought yours.'

The headlights of a car raked across the overlook, and Marsh swore under his breath.

'It's a police car,' Torey said in surprise.

He nodded. 'Of course. Coming out to break up any beer parties and send the juveniles home before they get into trouble. It's embarrassing, you know—I haven't been caught at a lover's lane since I was a kid.'

And it's all your fault. He hadn't said it, but she could almost hear him thinking it.

'Oh, Kimberley frowns on this sort of thing, does she?' Torey asked sweetly. I wonder, she thought, just what else Kimberley frowns on.

Torey sighed. That was foolish, she told herself. Once Kimberley was readmitted to her thoughts, the woman wasn't going to go away easily.

A burly officer came up to the car, torch in hand. 'Hi, Marsh,' he said genially. 'Everything all right?'

'Just fine. We are simply two consenting adults——'

Torey interrupted crisply. 'Who are watching the moon rise, officer.'

'In that case, better take her up to Sapphire Lake, Marsh.' The policeman walked away, swinging the torch jauntily, and Torey heard him chuckle.

Marsh started the engine a bit more violently than was necessary, and gravel spurted from under the tyres as the car headed back down the road. He shot a look at Torey. 'Watching the moon rise,' he said drily.

'Well, it was true.'

'*True* and *believable* are sometimes two different things,' he said. He pulled a handkerchief from his breast pocket and tossed it at her. 'When you've got lipstick smeared from ear to ear.'

'You look a bit wounded yourself.' She tugged the sun visor down and inspected herself in the lighted mirror on the back of it. It wasn't as bad as he seemed to think, but she wished that she had forgotten to fix her make-up at the country club while he went after the car. It would have been so much tidier in the end ... She rummaged for her lipstick in her handbag.

'Where's Sapphire Lake, anyway?' she asked. 'And what's so special about it?' She could feel the weight of his gaze, and she went on, without looking at him, 'Not that I'm suggesting we go, of course——'

'Why not?' He sounded almost affronted.

Torey reached for her lipstick and said primly, 'At the very least, we'd have to go home and get my car first.'

There was a split second of astounded silence, and then Marsh began to laugh. 'And a blanket,' he agreed.

'It's a great place to sit on the beach with a girl and a supply of hot toddies and——'

'This time of year? Not this girl,' Torey said with a shiver. But, if she was completely honest, she would have to admit the shiver was not all in anticipation of the cold sand.

'This time of year,' he insisted. 'With all the cabins empty, it's pitch-black out there. If the lake is still, there are stars all around you, even under the water. And when the moon rises it looks like some sort of pagan festival, with fingers of gold reaching out across the lake.' The sports car swung into their driveway and pulled up under the *porte cochère.* 'How about it? Shall we go?'

The temptation was incredible. Still, there was a nagging uncertainty which would not stop tugging at the back of her mind. Had he done it on purpose, planned to take her up to the Sentinel Oak, knowing how very likely it was that they would be seen there? He had even checked the clock.

For the time of moon-rise, she told herself, but she wasn't quite convinced; the doubt, once admitted to her mind, could not be banished.

Torey put the cap back on her lipstick with a snap and said, 'Sorry, but I forgot to tell you—my car wouldn't start at all today. So I'm afraid——'

'That's all right,' Marsh said earnestly. 'I know where one of my friends hides the key to his beachfront cabin.'

'That's not——' Then she saw the sparkle in his eyes and stopped abruptly. 'Goodnight, Marsh,' she said firmly. She got out and slammed the car door.

The same gentleman who had taken such good care of her at the country club lounged on the steps while she struggled with her key, and followed her inside. She didn't bother to take off her coat; she started straight for her room.

'Torey,' he called from the bottom of the stairs.

She turned on the landing and clenched her hands inside the pockets of her coat. He was leaning against the carved newel-post, looking up at her with a smile.

Oh, please, she whispered deep inside, but even she didn't quite know if she was asking for him to summon her back to his side, or leave her alone.

'It was fun tonight,' he said. 'If you should change your mind about Sapphire Lake——'

'You'll be the first to know,' she said quietly, and turned away from him.

Her room was a peaceful haven. She didn't even turn on any lights, just tossed her coat on the floor and dropped on to her bed.

'It was fun,' he had said. It was like a death knell, somehow. What had been quite literally the most important night of her life had been simple fun to him, a pleasant break in the routine of his life, a treat before settling down once again with Kimberley.

'It won't last,' Torey muttered into her pillow. 'He won't be happy with her. He couldn't be happy with someone who has so little sense of humour, so little spirit of fun.'

But that was not much comfort just now.

She lay there for a long time, trying to talk herself back into sanity. It's not your business, she told herself. If he ruins his life by marrying Kimberley, there's nothing anyone can do to stop him. And if you're thinking of hanging around just so you'll be there to pick up the pieces when the inevitable happens, you really need help, Torey Farrell!

She sat down at her drawing-table, finally, and turned on the light. It formed a little puddle of yellow through the long hours of the night as she drew, pouring out her heart on to the paper.

It was almost dawn when she put her pencil down amid the litter of the night's work and looked at the last sketch she had finished. It was fairly large, more detailed than most of her drawings, and it was split into three parts. In the first panel, crowds of party-goers milled around or sat by the fire in the big parlour of the house on Belle Vista, holding fluted glasses and nibbling snacks. One was a very elegant lady who was saying, 'How nice of you to invite us all over for champagne to celebrate the end of your marriage, Marsh.' It all looked very ordinary, very straightforward.

But the second panel was different. A tiny change of angle, a slightly wider view of the scene, and the party became a farce. The fluted glasses now appeared to have been sliced vertically down the middle. The plates were shattered shards. And the elegant lady, doing her best to keep her poise in the middle of the mess, even as she was trying to balance herself on a chair that had only two legs, went on calmly, 'I understand you had no trouble agreeing on a property settlement.'

'Not at all,' the man beside her replied breezily, as he offered her a choice of hors-d'oeuvre from a cast-iron skillet that had been sawed neatly in half.

And in the third panel, the view was of the outside of the house, as two men in hard hats held a measuring tape across the front veranda while a third stood by with a chainsaw, and from the window floated the rest of the host's comment, 'We agreed that we both wanted everything.'

Torey tossed the sketch into the pile on the foot of her bed and yawned. What good was this doing, she asked herself, sitting here speculating about the break-up of a hypothetical marriage, and what a man might do when he found himself suddenly single again?

'He'd probably move back into that town-house complex along with a lot of other swinging singles,' she muttered, 'and they'd all practise their neuroses together.'

She stopped abruptly and thought about it for a long time, and then shook her head. 'You can't be serious,' she told herself. 'You can't possibly draw a strip about a divorced man. You've got no experience.'

On the other hand, she'd certainly known her share of men whose marriages had dissolved. And she didn't have to confine herself to a divorced male, either; the concept of a housing complex for single people left her with all sorts of variations to draw on. And she did know an awful lot about being single...

'And it looks as if that state of affairs could go on for a long time,' she muttered, and then issued orders to stop feeling sorry for herself and get down to work.

She pulled another sheet of paper out of the package and began to sketch as fast as she could. Images were attacking her like a swarm of hornets, and she was drawing only rough bits, just enough to knock a gag out of the air and skewer it like an insect on a display-board, so that she could go back and study it all later.

That done, she began dragging out every line she had drawn in the last three months, to see how it all might fit together. And seeing those drawings again sparked other ideas, which had to be captured and sketched...

It was almost sunrise when she fell into bed, and she didn't even hear Marsh taking his shower. In fact, she wondered when the doorbell's peal dragged her out of a dream—she'd been standing in front of a huge crowd of applauding cartoonists, accepting an award for the best new strip of the year—who on earth would have the nerve to ring the bell in the middle of the night. Then she saw the clock on the corner of her drawing-table, and groaned, and decided not to answer it at all. The odds were that it was only someone selling magazines, anyway.

But whoever was on the veranda was persistent, and ultimately Torey dragged herself out of bed, pulled on yesterday's jeans and a brightly printed shirt, shoved her feet into running shoes, and combed her hair with her fingers on the way down the stairs.

Two business-like women were waiting, one carrying a bucket, the other with a tissue-covered bundle in her hands. Torey had just opened her mouth to explain to them that she hadn't ordered a cleaning service, so they were obviously at the wrong house, when one of them said, 'We're here to finish your wallpaper.'

Of course, Torey thought. With her ankle out of commission, Dolores can't help, but she's too much of a lady to leave me in a mess like this. And she certainly knows I'm incapable of finishing the job by myself. Bless her heart.

The woman carrying the tissue-covered bundle thrust it at Torey. 'The florist's delivery truck came while we were waiting,' she said.

Torey turned the pot around. Stapled to the tissue, out in the open for the world to see, was a card. 'Victoria Farrell, 600 Belle Vista,' it said in bold black letters, and below that a single, half-scrawled initial, 'M.' It was perfectly innocent, and also probably more damning, Torey thought, than anything else he could have written. When a man sent flowers with no indication of the reason...

She cast a glance at the two paper-hangers. There couldn't be much doubt in their minds about what had happened here last night—Torey stumbling to the door, obviously just out of bed, and getting flowers. At least, she thought, Marsh hadn't sent a thank-you card. That would have been the last straw!

It was a pot of daffodils, just coming into bloom, their brilliant yellow trumpet-like blossoms dewy and fresh. 'Obviously I'm not the type he sends roses to,' she muttered, and set the flowers on the kitchen counter, out of the way of comment.

She had just started up to her room to look at last night's work, half afraid of finding that it had not been inspired at all but simply another false start, when Gus and another burly man came bumping down the stairs carrying the claw-footed bath.

'I didn't know you were here today,' Torey said, without thinking. 'Oh—Marsh must have let you in.' Well, she thought, at least there are two people in town who know I didn't spend the night in Marsh's bedroom: Gus and his new helper. 'Where are you taking that tub, anyway?'

'Out. Mr. Endicott's orders.'

'Oh.' It gave her a sad sort of sinking feeling in the pit of her stomach. 'I suppose the heart-shaped whirlpool goes in this afternoon.'

'Not that I know of.'

She thought that one over while they manoeuvred the bath out of the front door. Surely Marsh would have checked out the idea with the plumber. And he must be intending something of the sort, or he wouldn't be exiling the old bath.

Then Gus said over his shoulder, 'Takes a while for those special-order numbers, you know. They don't make 'em every day.'

'Of course,' Torey muttered. She thought she heard one of the paper-hangers say something to the other one about decadent bathrooms, and she retreated to her own room in disarray.

The stack of cartoons on her drawing-table was still as thick, and—she thought—just as funny, as touching, as tender as they had seemed in the middle of the night. In one night, she had cut through the roadblock and come up with fully half of the ideas it would take for the strip's first thirteen weeks. Not that the work was done, by any means—the actual drawing of a single strip could sometimes take days. But the hardest part was out of the way.

If the syndicate agreed, she told herself sombrely. If they, too, liked the concept. If her ideas and her gags passed muster.

Don't be such a pessimist, she ordered. You already know they like your drawing style, and your cynical sense of humour. It's only the story-line that's in doubt.

She stared at the stack of drawings for a while and then gathered them into a bundle, told the paper-hangers to lock the door if they finished before she returned, and went out to her car. She hadn't been exaggerating when she'd told Marsh about its odd behaviour, but today it was a bit more co-operative and started after only a few minutes of coaxing.

Marsh's secretary showed her in without hesitation, after a single sidelong glance at the contents of the small box Torey was holding very carefully in both hands.

It was a big, square room, panelled in warm cherry-wood, with landscapes on the walls—a restful, efficient office. Kimberley ought to sack Sterling Granville, she thought, and let Marsh do the decorating. Didn't the woman recognise good taste at all?

He was just picking up the telephone, but he waved at a chair nearby. Torey leaned over his desk to set the box precisely in the middle of the blotter, and Marsh put the telephone down. 'What's this?' he asked.

'At the ice-cream shop they call it Devil's Delight— because it's all chocolate and sinfully rich, I suppose— and you can't make me believe that someone who thinks fudge frosting is a health food has stayed above this little concoction.'

'I haven't. I love these things.' He reached for the plastic spoon she'd brought, and dipped into the whipped-cream topping. 'I meant, why are you bringing me one?'

'A birthday present.'

'Torey,' he said softly, and put the spoon down. 'It's very sweet, but——'

'I should hope so—it's the most sickeningly sweet thing I could find. It's also a bribe. Do you have a fax machine?'

'What if I don't?'

'Then I take your Devil's Delight and go home.'

'It's right down the hall. Why?'

She hesitated. She was asking a sizeable favour, she reminded herself, and told the truth. 'I want to get some of my stuff to the syndicate for approval, and time is important.'

'You haven't been sending it as you go?' He savoured another bite, a chunk of double-chocolate cake dripping with hot fudge sauce. 'And I've been watching the mail all this time for nothing,' he mused. 'What's in it for me?'

'What else do you want? You're halfway through the Devil's Delight——' She stopped. 'Oh, come on, Marsh. You're not trying to negotiate anything Neanderthal, are you?'

'Like dragging you off to my cave? I hadn't thought of that, but it would have its attractions.' He dug into the dessert again. 'Are you suggesting I try it?'

Torey caught herself watching his tongue as he cleaned a stray bit of chocolate from the corner of his mouth. She very deliberately looked over his shoulder and out of the window to the highway and said, 'Of course not. What did you have in mind?'

'To see the cartoons,' he said promptly.

She glared at him.

'No editorial comments. I just want to make sure my fax machine won't be offended at what it's being asked to transmit.'

'If the average newspaper in the country can print the things, Marsh...'

He polished off the Devil's Delight and licked the spoon and looked meaningfully at the portfolio on her lap. 'Then I'm certainly mature enough to see them,' he suggested helpfully.

There was no winning an argument with the man; he was like quicksilver. 'Oh, all right,' Torey said crossly. 'It doesn't matter to me what you think!' She yanked the portfolio open and tossed the stack of drawings on to his desk blotter, barely missing the gooey container. Then she waited for him to comment about the roughness of the ideas and the obviously unfinished state of the drawings.

But he didn't. Instead he looked at each page so slowly and thoughtfully that Torey thought she would go mad before he finished. She finally flung herself out of her chair and paced the floor till she ended up standing at the window, staring out at nothing, every nerve-end screaming.

It's supposed to be funny, dammit, she wanted to yell at him. Can't you at least chuckle—just once?

'Well?' she said finally. 'Go ahead—tell me you hate it.'

'I wonder why you would want to hear that,' he mused. 'I think it's very good. I like your characters, I like your style, I like your story——'

She turned from the window. 'You didn't laugh,' she said uncertainly.

'So it does matter to you what I think,' he said softly.

She bowed her head a little, and tears stung her eyes.

Marsh came across the room, quickly. 'I'm sorry, Torey—I shouldn't tease you like that. What really matters is the syndicate's opinion, so run along and get these on their way. My secretary will show you.'

She didn't look at him. She gathered up the pages and shoved them back into the portfolio, and was almost to the door when he spoke again.

'Tell me something, Torey.' She stopped, but she didn't turn around, and he said, 'If I had gone Neanderthal on you, what would you have done?'

She bit her lip and smiled a little. 'Thanks for letting me use the fax, Marsh.' And she thought, I would have dragged myself into your cave, that's what I would have done...

CHAPTER NINE

TOREY didn't get an immediate answer, of course, and she hadn't expected one; photofax could duplicate a piece of paper anywhere across the country in a matter of seconds, but getting a group of people to look at that piece of paper and make a decision based on it was sometimes another thing altogether. She comforted herself with the knowledge that she had now done everything she could, and she knew that the best thing to do was go home and finish off the first few strips. It would help pass the time faster.

She had every intention of going home to work, but after ten minutes of coaxing she realised that this time her car really was dead. She got out and kicked it, which didn't do any good and only made her toes hurt.

Marsh called from halfway across the car park, 'Don't you dare do that again!'

He must have been watching from his office window, she thought. It gave her a warm sort of twinge to know that he'd been looking out for her, but she didn't want to admit it. 'Why?' she asked crisply. 'Is there a law against abusing stubborn mechanical objects?'

'There ought to be. I don't want to spend another evening in the X-ray waiting-room, thanks.' He was still zipping his coat, and he wrinkled his nose at the smell of raw petrol as he came up to the car. 'Well, you've flooded it properly now. Hasn't anyone ever taught you how to start a car in cold weather?'

'There's a special way?'

He groaned. 'Well, it's a little late for lessons now.'

'You mean it's permanently dead?'

'Unfortunately, no,' he mused. He stepped back and looked at the rust around the wheels, at the battered chrome trim, and the long crease in the driver's door, and sighed.

'Don't blame that dent on me,' Torey said defensively. 'I was side-swiped on the freeway right before I left LA, and I didn't have time or money to get it fixed.'

Marsh muttered something under his breath, and then said, 'A mercy killing might be in order. You've already applied all the gasoline it would take to give the poor thing a decent cremation. All you need is a match.'

She ignored that. 'So what do I do?'

'It'll have to sit for an hour or so before you can try again.'

'Great,' she said sarcastically. 'I did have a few other plans, but——'

'I'll take you home.'

She walked across the car park beside him and ran a hand over the slick, newly polished surface of his sports car while she waited for him to dig his keys out of his pocket. There was not even a trace of gravel dust from last night; he must have had it washed this morning. 'You could just let me take your car,' she said demurely, 'and you could bring mine home after work tonight.'

'On the other hand,' Marsh mused, 'a brisk walk would do you good, Victoria. It's only about five miles from here to the house.'

'It's very sweet of you to give me a ride,' Torey murmured.

Marsh grinned. 'I thought you might see it that way.' He opened the passenger door with a flourish for her.

It was different, being beside him in daylight, without the compelling romantic spell of the moon and the stars and the Sentinel Oak. But she couldn't help thinking about last night, and the heart-stopping magic of being in his arms, of kissing him...

And what about Marsh? she thought. What was he feeling today?

'Thank you for the daffodils,' she offered finally.

He smiled a little, but he didn't comment. The car pulled up under the *porte cochère*. 'I'll start your car after a while and have someone bring it home,' he said. 'Want to try the Chinese restaurant tonight? They do some exciting things with scallops, I understand.'

'If you like,' she said, trying to sound as if it didn't matter. And it didn't, she admitted. If he'd suggested they sit around an igloo and chew on a raw seal, she would probably have agreed.

His gloved hand brushed her cheek lightly, but she thought his mind was elsewhere—probably back at the warehouse, catching up on the work she had interrupted. She stood on the step and watched until the car went out of sight a couple of blocks down Belle Vista, and then she went inside.

The paper-hangers had finished. The smell of wallpaper paste hung heavily in the big parlour, and smears of the stuff still decorated the woodwork. But it was astounding what a change it made in the room to have a fresh, clean surface, to have soft flowers to look at instead of livid blotches and faded, peeling old paper.

'I didn't realise it bothered me so much,' Torey told herself, looking at the spot above the mantel where the discoloration had been the harshest. She had always admired the proportions of this room, but she had never been very comfortable here. Now it was like walking into a garden; it invited her to hang just the right print above the mantel, and then to pull a chair around next to the fire, and pick up a good book.

She should ignore the lure and go to work, she told herself. But the fact was, she was already nearly cross-

eyed from working all night. What more could she hope
to accomplish, she thought, in her current state of ex-
haustion? Wouldn't it be better to wait till she had had
some rest?

She pushed the plastic covering off Marsh's white
leather couch and sat down.

At least have the good taste to be honest with yourself,
Torey Farrell, she ordered. You're not so much interested in placing your comfortable chair by the fire as
you are with showing Marsh what this house could be
like, and how nice it would be to have a little woman
around who doesn't have her mind set on silver watered
silk and clouded ceilings.

And what, she asked herself, was so awfully wrong
about that philosophy? She had certainly never promised
to help him get Kimberley back; indeed, she had told
him quite clearly that she was only interested in the
benefits his scheme held for her. She wasn't bound by
any sort of pledge. She didn't have to sit quietly in a
corner in the hope that some day he would notice her.
She was free to take action. Still——

'If something is worth having,' she told herself stoutly,
'it is worth fighting for.' What kind of chicken-hearted
defeatist was she, anyway, with this idea of surrendering
before the battle was even fought? If she truly wanted
Marsh Endicott, what was so wrong with going after
him?

And in any case, the little voice at the back of her
brain asked, what have you got to lose? Not much, that's
sure. The only evidence you've got that he even finds
you attractive is a couple of passionate kisses, and you
asked for both of those incidents yourself. Can we stop
and look at the view, indeed! What else was the man
supposed to do?

She tried her best to ignore that taunt, and went up
to the attic. She had never done any sort of systematic

survey of Violet's furniture. She told herself that that was all she was doing today—just looking. She certainly couldn't haul that stuff down three flights of stairs by herself.

Most of it wasn't worth it, anyway. She shivered a little as she climbed over a sofa, a massive, overstuffed style upholstered in vivid purple damask. It must weigh five hundred pounds. Carry it downstairs? She'd be lucky if she could push it out of her way!

But when she found the Victorian parlour set, with its carved walnut chair-frames and almost-perfect wine-red velvet upholstery, tucked into a far corner of the attic-room and covered with an old white sheet, she had to bring a chair down just to see what it would look like against the new wallpaper. That called for a small marble-topped table to set beside it, and the hurricane lamp she'd found draped in cobwebs and tucked away under the eaves.

Time slipped away as she worked, and she didn't know how long Marsh had been leaning against the dining-room door watching before she saw him. She was whistling a soft little tune as she polished the carved sofa-table that she had just wrestled into place by the wide front window, and when she turned to pick up her bottle of furniture cleaner he was there. Her whistle broke off in the middle of a note.

He's so very good-looking, she thought, and remembered the first time she had seen him, in this room. If I had known then, she thought, that this man would become everything to me, what would I have done? Would I have gone straight back to my car and started for California once more? It would probably have been the sensible thing to do...

'I thought for a minute that Violet was back,' he said.

She looked around uncertainly at the eclectic mix of furniture. The white leather couch was turned at a right

angle to the fireplace now, with the glass table in front
of it neatly centred on an old oriental rug that had been
rolled up in the attic's cedar closet. Opposite the couch
were a pair of skirted Victorian chairs, their upholstery
a bit worn and faded, but still usable. And around the
room there were other chairs, hassocks, tables—she
hadn't realised till now, seeing it through his eyes, just
how many marauding trips she had made to the attic
this afternoon. No wonder her whole body was aching.

'Too much?' she asked.

Marsh shook his head. 'Not if you're planning to start
a furniture showroom. Just leave an aisle here and there,
Torey, so your customers can get through.'

She stuck her tongue out at him. 'What are you doing
here already, anyway?'

'Already?' He glanced at his wristwatch. 'I'm late, as
a matter of fact. Too many interruptions today.'

That puts you in your place, Torey, she told herself.
'Well, my car hasn't arrived yet.'

'Oh—your car.'

'You were going to have it delivered,' she reminded.

'I didn't forget about it,' he said defensively. 'It still
wouldn't start.'

She didn't know whether to groan—the last thing she
needed right now was another repair bill—or to laugh
at his obvious discomfort. So his mechanical diagnosis
hadn't been correct after all; apparently it wasn't just a
simple trick of how to start the engine.

'I called the garage to come and pick it up.'

'Great,' Torey muttered. 'A towing bill on top of the
cost of repairs.'

'I thought they should see the problem in its raw state.
Besides, you'll be swimming in money once The Swingles
gets going.' He sat down on the couch, picked up an
apple from the bowl she had painstakingly arranged on

the glass coffee-table, and bit into it. The apple split with a juicy crack. 'What did you say?'

'Nothing.' If I wanted him to stay out of the fruit bowl, Torey told herself, I should have used wax apples. 'The Swingles? What are you talking about?'

'Your cartoon strip. You didn't tell me its name.'

'Because it doesn't have one yet.'

'Oh, that explains it. At any rate, I was thinking about it this afternoon. It's full of swinging singles, and I thought—The Swingles. Why not?'

She tried it out, turning it over and over on her tongue. 'I like it,' she announced.

'Well, don't sound so astonished. Of course you like it.'

It irritated her. 'Don't get arrogant, Marsh—I certainly wouldn't name my strip something I hated just because you thought it up!'

'You wouldn't?' He sounded disappointed. 'In that case, I won't tell you any of my other ideas.'

'Good!'

'I got scarcely any work done this afternoon because of it, you know. And then when I get home I find you haven't given the thing a thought. It isn't fair.' He picked through the fruit bowl again and selected a banana. 'I suppose you want me to help move furniture next.'

There was the love-seat that completed the parlour set . . . No, she thought. Better to leave it right where it was. 'I wouldn't dare ask you,' she said frankly. But then she saw the sparkle in his eyes, and she knew she'd been had again. She shrugged her aching shoulders and rubbed the back of her neck, which felt as if someone had braided the muscles. 'When is there going to be a functional bathtub in this house again, Marsh? I could certainly enjoy soaking tonight.'

'I haven't talked to Gus lately.' To her disappointment, he didn't offer an explanation of why the bath had been removed from the house altogether. Instead, he folded the banana peel neatly and laid it on the corner of the coffee-table, then came across the parlour to her. 'But I'll tell you what—just scream when you get in the shower, and I'll come up and scrub your back.'

'I'd scream, all right,' Torey said, trying to keep her voice light and not think about how pleasant that sounded.

'It's as good as a massage.' He suited actions to words, turning her away from him and starting to rub her shoulders. Those big hands of his were even stronger than they looked, she found herself thinking after a few seconds; the soothing pressure against her aching muscles seemed to be effortless for him. She let her head droop as her neck muscles relaxed.

'Good lord, even the back of your neck is tempting,' Marsh muttered. His fingers didn't stop rubbing, tracing and stroking each separate muscle, but suddenly his mouth touched the very nape of her neck, where the blonde hair had slipped to the side. His lips were warm and soft against her skin, and for Torey—who had never thought of the back of her neck as a particularly erogenous zone—it was something of a surprise to feel darts of pleasure rising there and striking off on random paths, as unpredictable as static electricity, till every cell of her body was aglow.

She must have made some sort of noise—a little protesting moan, perhaps—because he suddenly let her go and said, almost roughly, 'Sometimes I think I need my head examined.'

Torey put a hand out to the fluted post beside her for support.

'Take your time in getting ready,' he added, and turned away to pick up the evening newspaper. 'We don't need reservations at the Chinese place.'

'Do you think that's such a good idea?' she said. It came out in sort of a jagged whisper. 'Maybe we shouldn't go at all, Marsh——'

'And stay at home instead?' He smiled ruefully, but it didn't quite reach his eyes. 'I doubt that would be safer, Torey. In fact, I'd almost guarantee it.'

She bit her lip to keep from saying, What makes you so sure I want to be safe? and climbed the stairs, telling herself not to be a fool. 'Don't confuse the fact that he's physically attracted to you with the idea that it might be anything more than that,' she told herself firmly. 'Only a starry-eyed idiot would get herself into that trap.'

The lecture didn't help much, and the shower didn't either; she kept thinking about his offer to scrub her back, and caught herself more than once wondering just what would happen if she leaned out the bathroom door and called his name. Finally she swore at herself and turned the shower down to an icy mist. It helped a little.

The Chinese restaurant was at the edge of town, part of a shopping mall complex that Torey hadn't seen before. It was decorated in garish red and black; even the interior walls were red enamel, but the brilliance was softened by the art objects and oddities that were hanging against it.

'They've redecorated,' Marsh said, with a long look around.

'Obviously Sterling Granville didn't do it,' Torey muttered.

'Elementary, my dear. No clouded ceiling.' He held her chair and then sat down across the table, rather than next to her. Torey was vaguely disappointed.

The waitress arrived with menus and a pot of fragrant tea, and poured it into cups not much larger than thimbles. Torey sipped hers and looked down the long and confusing list of dishes, and said, determined not to let herself forget that things were not the way she would like them to be, 'Is he really French?'

'Of course not. He was raised near the stockyards in Omaha, Nebraska. That's a state secret, of course.'

'Why? Are you planning to blackmail him?'

He smiled approvingly. 'Clever girl.'

In other words, Torey thought, I can stop worrying about the silver drawing-room; there really won't be one.

A tray of appetisers appeared between them, and he dipped a fried won ton in sweet and sour sauce and crunched it with relish. 'As long as they keep these coming, I don't care about the rest,' he said. He set his menu aside and raised his teacup. 'To your new strip, Victoria.'

She smiled and joined in the toast. 'And its new name—thank you, Marsh.'

'Ah, yes, the name—I was meaning to ask you why it didn't have one before.' It was bland and innocent, but there was a note in his voice that warned her to be cautious.

She stared at the glossy black surface of the table and drank most of her cup of tea before she said, gently, 'I just hadn't found the right one yet.'

'Just where did the inspiration come from, anyway?' he asked. He sounded honestly curious, but then he added, softly, 'And when?'

Her gaze lifted to meet his, her eyes widening a little. It doesn't matter when I got the idea, she told herself. The timing isn't important, really. It certainly should mean nothing to him...So why is he asking?

Over Marsh's shoulder she saw a familiar form outside the glass wall at the front of the restaurant. 'There's Stan!' she exclaimed, and started to wave.

Instantly she realised that Marsh had heard the relief in her voice, and the tell-tale colour of embarrassment began to rise in her cheeks, like a reflection of her delicate shell-pink sweater.

Marsh laughed and pushed his chair back as Stan came up to the table. 'Are you eating Chinese tonight?' he asked. 'We've only reached the appetiser stage if you'd like to join us.'

Torey told herself it was silly to wish that he hadn't issued the invitation; if he hadn't, she'd have done it herself.

Without a second of hesitation, Stan pulled up the chair between them.

'We were just discussing where great ideas come from,' Marsh went on smoothly. 'You know, those strokes of genius that come now and then.'

Stan looked around for the waitress. 'Sounds pretty lofty to me.'

'And you're supposed to be the intellectual of the crowd,' Marsh said mournfully. 'I'm disappointed in you, Stan.' He refilled Torey's cup and added, 'I've always wanted to ask some of you creative types just where the lightning strikes originate, Torey.'

Stan finished giving his order and said, 'I'm glad to see you're getting out of the house, Marsh.'

Marsh's eyebrows went up a fraction. 'Have I been ill or something?'

'I heard about Kimberley,' Stan explained, and shook his head mournfully.

Marsh crunched another won ton. 'Thank you for your condolences, dear boy. Torey——'

'But I *didn't* say I was sorry about it,' Stan assured him earnestly. 'I said I'm glad you're not moping around the house, or threatening to do something silly.'

'Like trying to get her back?' Torey asked sweetly.

Marsh glared at both of them, impartially.

Torey couldn't help it. She started to giggle.

Stan laughed, too. Then he said, 'She's joking, Marsh—isn't she?'

Marsh put his elbows on the table and leaned his forehead on his interlaced fingers, almost as if he were meditating. Finally, he said, 'All right, Torey—I can see further than my nose, and I concede that you win this round. If you'll let Kimberley have a rest for the night, I won't ask you about the strip just now——'

'Strip?' Stan sounded horrified.

'As in cartoons,' Marsh said, as if he were instructing a child. '*Not* as in topless bars.'

That sent Torey off once more. She started to laugh, tried to smother the sound in her napkin, and ended up dabbing tears from her eyes. Marsh met her eyes with astonishment, held out for a second longer, and also burst into mirth.

There was a little knife-edged pain in her heart as she watched him laugh, and she twisted her napkin in her lap and wished that he could really be hers, for always, to share this sense of the absurd, to share—everything.

How very much I love him, she thought. And then she wanted to cry in earnest.

But that was impossible; it would cause too many questions. So she kept laughing instead, guiding the conversation into light-hearted channels, teasing Marsh, tormenting Stan, dancing away from any hint of serious subjects.

But when dinner was over and Marsh invited Stan to come back to the house with them, the bubble of laughter burst inside her, and left her feeling flat and depressed and tired. For she knew why he had done it; it would be safer that way...

She sat curled up on the end of the leather couch, her feet under her, her head against a cushion, a glass of wine in her hand, and let her mind drift while the two of them dissected city politics. But she was wide awake enough when Stan said goodnight, and added, 'I'll leave you to your ghosts. It would drive me nuts to hear Violet clanking around the house like that.'

She listened for a moment, and shook her head. 'No, that's just the radiators talking to themselves. Violet's only in the plumbing.'

'You can say that again,' Marsh added, under his breath.

Stan laughed and kissed her cheek.

Marsh saw him to the door. When he came back to the parlour he stood at the end of the couch for a long moment, looking down at her, and a deep uneasiness began to stir in the pit of Torey's stomach. Surely he didn't think she expected——

She sat up a little straighter and began to gather their wine glasses and napkins together on to the snack tray, being very careful to keep one eye on him.

'Torey,' he said finally.

She had kicked her shoes off long before, and now she could find only one of them under the coffee-table. She made a frantic, fumbling search as Marsh came closer, and finally gave it up. 'I'll just take these glasses to the kitchen and——' You're babbling, she told herself. She jumped up from the couch and reached for the tray.

Marsh's hand closed on her wrist. It was a gentle hold, but she wouldn't have bet anything on her ability to break free. 'I'll clear up the mess,' he said.

'Then goodnight, Marsh——'

'Stan got a kiss,' he reminded softly.

'That was a little diff——' She stopped abruptly and bit her tongue hard.

Marsh smiled. 'A little different? Yes, it certainly was. What happened, Torey? Why are you so shy all of a sudden?'

'I thought you didn't want this to happen,' she whispered.

He had captured her other wrist as well, and he was drawing her gently, inexorably, towards him. 'I have wanted to do this all evening,' he said softly. He released her wrists and raised one hand to her chin, turning her face up to his.

'But you invited Stan,' she said uncertainly.

'That was my last crumb of common sense, and in less than two minutes I was regretting it. Damn Stan, anyway; I thought the man was never going to go home.' His eyes were darker than she had ever seen them before. 'Torey——' His mouth was soft against hers, and yet there was a suppressed fierceness about the way he kissed her, as if he was fighting for control.

It would take very little to fan that spark into an explosion, she thought dimly, even as she relaxed against him, letting herself slacken and almost melt to fit the hard contours of his body. His hands were splayed across the small of her back, holding her firmly against him, and the warmth crept from his fingers through her spine and gathered at the very centre of her, like a Bunsen burner whose flame was slowly, carefully, being turned higher.

'Watching you, the way you were just sitting there— you have no idea what it did to me,' he whispered against her lips. Then, as if mere words could not express what he wanted to say, he kissed her again, more urgently, his tongue exploring the soft mysteries of her mouth, telling her what he wanted, what he needed...

She made a little moaning noise in her throat and fitted herself even more closely against him. His hands slid up under her sweater, caressing the soft flesh, finding their way surely to cup her breasts. The warmth of his thumbs against the soft nipples seemed to reduce her bra to nothing more than illusion.

She could feel herself unfolding like a flower, welcoming him, wanting more. You're not thinking clearly, Torey, she told herself. You're actually considering going to bed with him.

That was a joke, she thought. 'Considering' was scarcely the word; it implied logical thought. But there was no reason involved in this, no rational judgement. Just feelings.

Marsh seemed to read her thoughts. 'The hell with common sense,' he said huskily. 'I want to make love with you, Torey.'

Why shouldn't I? she asked herself. Why should I fight what I want so badly?

Because you'll regret it in the morning, the obnoxious little voice at the back of her brain announced.

The hesitation in her had communicated itself to him. His hands were still under her sweater, but they slid slowly back over her sensitive ribs to rest firmly at her waist, and he held her a little way from him. 'Better get out while you can,' he warned. His voice was almost hoarse. 'Or I'm likely to drag you upstairs by the hair and rape you.'

She felt cold, held away from him like that; the only two spots of warmth in her body were where his hands still rested.

If I go to bed with him, she thought, I may regret it in the morning. Or I may not. But if I don't—then I will surely regret it for all my life...

She shook her head, slowly. 'Not rape,' she said, very quietly.

'You don't think I'm capable of it?' He gave a harsh laugh. 'Torey, don't be foolish. Any man——'

'It wouldn't be rape, Marsh.'

He exhaled suddenly, as if all the breath had been forced from him, and said, 'Are you certain of that?'

She nodded, and raised her hands to his shoulders, and locked her fingers at the back of his neck, and stood on her toes to press herself against him. 'It can't be,' she pointed out logically, 'if that's what both of us want.'

He looked down at her for one aeons-long instant, and then he kissed her temple, her ear, her throat, her lips, as if the hunger that drove him demanded that he taste every accessible inch of her.

And when he took her hands and led her up the stairs, she did not hesitate, even though she knew that this would turn her world upside-down, and that nothing would ever again be quite the same.

CHAPTER TEN

THE master bedroom had not changed much since Torey had moved out of it. Marsh's king-sized bed took up a great deal more of the room than her smaller one had, of course, but apart from the black leather chair beside the fireplace he hadn't bothered with other furniture. The prints she had so carefully chosen for this room were now hanging in her new bedroom; he had not replaced them. In fact, the walls were bare, with one exception.

Beside the front window, in the corner where her drawing-board had stood, there was now an old, battered frame, hung at a slight angle so that the caricature of him which she had drawn on the wallpaper was perfectly aligned within it.

Seeing it there tickled Torey's sense of humour, and touched her heart as well. Her last doubt—the final nagging suspicion that what she was doing was incredibly foolish—vanished, and she turned to Marsh and held out her arms.

When he came to her, she let her palms rest for an instant against the soft linen of his shirt, feeling the strong pulsing of his heart under her hands, and then she started to carefully unfasten his buttons, working from the top down, concentrating on each one as if it were the only important thing in the world. When she was finished, he shrugged out of the shirt and kissed her lightly—a kiss that for all its apparent casualness was somehow more arousing than any that had gone before—and then gently began to remove her clothes. He was as slow and careful as any lady's maid, and by the time her sweater and trousers were neatly folded in a heap Torey was quivering with the sensual pleasure that his touch aroused.

He had told her he was capable of violence, and she had no reason to doubt him, but there was not so much as a hint of it in him then. He held her, caressed her, aroused her, exploring her body with such precise persistence that she was nearly sobbing with eagerness in a matter of minutes. For Torey, it was a lesson that was almost painful in its intensity. She had not known until today that the nape of her neck was a sensual zone, but that, she realised, was only the beginning. Every spot on her body was erogenous when it was Marsh who was exploring, and she cried out and writhed against him, desperate for relief from the delicious torment he was causing.

Only then did his control begin to slip, undermined by her impatience. It was a lapse that Torey was only too happy to assist. She pulled him down to her, begging, pleading with every cell for their mutual satisfaction, and he answered the demands of her body with his own. They moved together in perfect rhythms that only lovers knew, and together they slipped over the edge of the world and into infinity, spinning out of control through the blackness of space, without concern for how or when they might find their way back to earth again.

The first thing she was really aware of, once the universe had settled back on to its foundations again, was the warmth of his breath brushing against the hollow between her breasts, and the soft scrape of his stubbly cheek on her tender skin as he raised his head to look down at her. 'Victoria,' he said, hoarsely. It sounded almost like a question.

His hair was an incredible tangle of curls. She smoothed it down with more care than was strictly necessary, loving the soft silkiness of it against her palms, and answered him with a kiss.

He smiled then, and twisted around until he was propped up against the pillows and she lay against him, her cheek teased by the soft dark hair that formed a mat on his chest. Her ear was against his heart, and she listened to the slowing beat, lulled almost to sleep by its hypnotic regularity and by the comfort of his arms.

If only, she thought, it could always be like this...

She woke at dawn, and it took a few seconds for her to remember where she was. The unfamiliar feel of the mattress, the foreign way the shadows seemed to fall across the bed, the unaccustomed softness of a satin sheet sliding across her bare skin, instead of the rough linen variety that Violet had seemed to favour.

Funny, she thought. Marsh didn't seem the sort to indulge himself in satin sheets. Always prepared, she told herself. That ought to be his motto.

She turned, cautiously, to look at him. He looked as if he was worried; there were frown lines between his eyes. Or perhaps it was just the first rays of morning light falling across his pillow, for his stirred suddenly and muttered something and turned towards her, tossing one arm across her and pulling her, effortlessly, against him. The result seemed to please him, for he smiled a little and snuggled his face into her hair.

'Great,' she muttered. 'Now I'm a teddy bear.'

'Torey bear,' he said, distinctly.

She twisted around as best she could and stared at him suspiciously, but he looked perfectly innocent and absolutely dead to the world.

So he talks in his sleep, too, she thought. What a dandy surprise! Well, at least it was warm in his arms, she told herself, and she curled into a more comfortable position so that she could go back to sleep herself. It was almost without thought that she drew his hand up till his fingers nestled against the enticing curve of her breast.

A quiet chuckle tickled her ear, and his fingers moved, very slightly, against her nipple, transforming an innocent caress into a gently provocative stroking that sent waves of pleasure sluicing through her.

'Not fair,' she protested. 'You were asleep——'

'And you weren't.' He raised himself on one elbow and grinned at her, his fingers never slowing their sensual play. He kissed her softly, and whispered, 'Which means you asked for whatever you get.' Then his hand wandered down over her ribs and across her stomach, to stroke the soft flesh of her inner thigh, and he kissed her again, slowly and deeply. 'Unless you can convince me that you didn't know what you were doing.'

With darts of pleasure rocketing straight to the very core of her? With the hunger for him rising to a pitch even stronger than she had felt last night?

'I warn you,' he said against her lips, 'it will take some fancy talking to convince me that you really didn't mean to be seductive.'

'Then why should I bother to try?' It came out in a husky, enticing whisper, and Marsh growled and turned on to his back, dragging her with him until she was sprawled helplessly across him, leaving his hands free to work their dangerous magic, to turn her once more into a mindless creature capable only of feeling.

And only when the passion was satisfied did she tumble once more into exhausted oblivion, nestled close to him, with every breath he took seeming to serve her body, too.

It was with a profound sense of well-being that she roused again, much later, and found sunlight pouring across the big bed, its tangled sheets a mute reminder of the craziness of the night.

Marsh was gone. He's already at work, she thought, and wondered, with a half-smile, whether he'd have any luck keeping his mind on business. She thought, herself, that she'd be lucky today if she could concentrate on anything except him...

She lay there for a long moment, luxuriating in the pleasant afterglow, the soft sheets, the warm sunlight, and then reluctantly she pushed herself out of bed. She found a robe hanging on the back of the wardrobe door—a red and blue tartan plaid—and she rolled up the sleeves and hiked the waistline up to approximately the right level. It was big enough to wrap herself in twice over, and it smelled like Marsh's aftershave—which, she admitted, was the major attraction in wearing it.

She was still arranging the folds of the robe and inspecting herself in the long mirror on the bathroom door when she heard footsteps coming up the stairs. Her eyes went instantly to the clock. Perhaps it wasn't so late after all, and Marsh hadn't yet left the house. Or perhaps it was Gus coming to work, instead.

She gathered up her clothes in a single swoop and in her hurry to get out of the room practically collided with a large, solid male in the doorway. The impact almost knocked the breath out of her; she fell back against the door and looked up. 'Marsh,' she said. 'I thought you'd gone to work.'

He was wearing jeans, but he was barefoot, and he hadn't bothered to put on a shirt. It looked as if he had roused suddenly and rushed downstairs for something.

'Those sample books,' he said urgently. 'Where did you put them?'

The serious note in his voice startled her. 'Sample books?' she asked, momentarily at a loss.

From the landing, a cool, crisp voice said, 'Well, isn't this cosy?' and Kimberley leaned an elbow on the carved post at the turn of the stairs, as if she were prepared to stand there forever.

It was the doorbell that took him downstairs in such a hurry, Torey thought abruptly. And it must have been the doorbell that woke me, even though I didn't consciously hear it. Unless he was waiting for her, and she didn't have to ring the bell at all.

No, she thought. Not that. Surely not that. Kimberley came to get her books of fabric and wallpaper samples, that's all.

But, whatever had brought this confrontation about, it couldn't have been any more damning a picture, Torey thought. There she stood, in the doorway of Marsh's room, wearing his robe, her arms full of obviously feminine clothes, complete with lacy underthings peeking out from between the crumpled folds of her shell-pink sweater...

'Kimberley, you were not invited to come up here,' Marsh said firmly. He raked one hand through his hair, leaving it looking even more dishevelled.

Kimberley shrugged. 'I'm just looking at your view, Marsh.' She glanced out of the leaded glass window on the landing and then turned to stare up at Torey again. 'And what a view it is.'

'Dammit, Kimberley, will you listen to reason for one minute?'

Something inside Torey seemed to shrivel up and die then. Nothing had changed, after all, except that Marsh had got caught up in his own scheme, and he had let it get out of hand. If he no longer cared about Kimberley, he might have said any number of things to her then, but he would certainly not have pleaded for her to listen to reason.

She shot a look up at him, cautiously, through her lashes. He was staring at Kimberley, and he looked more miserable than she had ever seen a human being look.

And he deserves every wretched moment of it, she told herself vengefully. He asked for it. He used me, and I hate him for it.

But had she not volunteered to be used? And as for what had happened between them last night, had she not purposely closed her eyes to the truth. 'The hell with common sense', he had said. She had scarcely heard him at the time—she had not wanted to hear. But he had known what he was doing...

And as for hating him—was it possible to hate him, at the same time that her soul longed for him to be happy, at whatever cost to herself?

She didn't know. But she knew, now, just what wrenching pain it was possible to feel, and still remain standing upright. So this is what it feels like when a heart breaks, she thought. There was a searing pain screaming along each nerve.

She didn't look at him. 'Last night was a mistake, Marsh,' she said quietly. 'I'm sorry for it.' She stepped around him, careful not even to let her arm brush against his. Any contact at all would be too much to stand, she thought. 'Your sample books are in the window-seat right behind you,' she told Kimberley, and with her head high she went off, silent-footed, towards her own bedroom.

Something stopped her, halfway there, and forced her to turn and look back. Perhaps it was the hope that he would be watching her, wishing her back. But he was no longer at the top of the stairs. He had gone down to Kimberley.

My own foolishness, she thought. If I'd only left the damned sample books in the parlour yesterday—but no, I had to neaten the place up and put them out of sight!

And what difference would it have made? she asked herself. None, in the long run. If it hadn't been the sample books this morning, it would have been something else—today, tomorrow, some day soon. And another few days would have changed nothing—except, perhaps, that it would have been even harder on her if she had had a little more time to pretend.

What a fool you are, Torey Farrell, she told herself. He told you he was attracted to you, that's all. And what did it really mean, anyway? Certainly, he was ready for a good time, but how could you let yourself believe it was anything more than that?

She pulled on her jeans and sweater with trembling hands, and tied a bandanna over her hair.

He's going to pay for this, she thought. It is going to cost him royally.

It was some consolation to plot her revenge. Marsh would end up with his precious house, after all—she certainly wasn't going to stay around for any more of this kind of treatment! But she wasn't going to let it be cheap for him; he ought to pay, and he was going to have to. She would take the money and go back to California, and——

'Do what? Live happily ever after?' she asked herself wryly. 'That ought to be quite a challenge.' Without him, could she ever be quite happy again?

She idly flipped through the stack of cartoons on her drawing-table, the originals that she had dropped here yesterday after the photofaxes had gone off to Los Angeles. She didn't even really see them, but it provided a bit of comfort to touch these ordinary, down-to-earth things.

At the very bottom of the stack was the three-panel drawing of Marsh's divorce party. She pulled it out and stared at it long and thoughtfully. This had been the inspiration for the strip, but it had not been part of the set she had sent off to California. This drawing was far too personal for that.

Personal—it almost made her shudder to realise just how personal it was. If she took out the reference to marriage and divorce, it could fit Torey herself just as easily as it had Kimberley. Wasn't she doing precisely the same thing when she planned to force the price of the house higher? Wasn't she insisting on having more than her share, at whatever cost? Wasn't she, too, guilty of the kind of personal greed she had accused Kimberley of displaying?

And was it fair to blame Marsh for it all? He wanted a good time, and he thought that was all you wanted, too, she told herself. It wasn't his fault you fell in love.

Still, leaving was the only answer; it would be easier anywhere else on earth than it would be if she stayed here. She'd start packing today, she told herself firmly, and just as soon as she was ready she would load everything into her car, and leave Springhill by nightfall.

Her car—the one that wouldn't start. Her car—the one that had been towed off to some garage, heaven only knew where.

She groaned. It felt as if a trap had just closed around her. Without that car...

She could ask Marsh about it, she supposed, but she didn't want to talk to him just now—not until she had control of herself. Until she could face up to his explanation, or—equally likely—his unwillingness to discuss the situation at all, with calmness, there was no point in talking at all.

Suddenly the house was a stifling pit, a narrow, dark cave that was threatening to fall in on her at any moment. She grabbed a windbreaker and slipped down the back stairs and out of the kitchen door as if she were being pursued. She didn't listen for voices in the parlour; she was too afraid of what she might hear.

She walked for what seemed miles, through sections of Springhill that she had never been through before, and that—now—she knew she would never see again. But there was no room in her mind to mourn that at the moment, even though she knew that she would miss this little town. In just a few weeks she had come to enjoy the town, the people, the relaxed pace. Some day, she would regret having to leave it. But for now...

She put her head down, and her hands in her pockets, and walked on.

She finally found herself in the cemetery, skirting the last patches of stubborn snow to make her way to Violet's grave. Odd, she thought, that her subconscious mind would have brought her here. Or perhaps it wasn't strange at all. Violet, too, had had her troubles when it came to love. If she had loved her husband, and had felt herself to be the cause of his estrangement from his family, what a dreadful feeling that must have been. And if she hadn't loved him, or if he had not loved her... Well, Torey thought, in its own way, that would have been even worse, to know that she was no substitute at all for the son he had lost.

There were flowers at the base of Violet's tombstone, tucked away in the shadow of the granite, almost hidden to anyone but a careful observer. Torey brushed a couple of dead oak leaves off the stone and sat down on the corner of it, looking thoughtfully down at the red and white blooms. Carnations—half a dozen of them, surrounded by greenery, tied with a white ribbon.

They had been there for a day or two at least, she thought; the flowers were tired-looking, as if the cold nights had drained their vitality. The green ferns that formed a blanket for the blooms had curled up as if shivering. Only the ribbon remained unaffected.

I should have brought her flowers myself, she thought. It's only now that I can really begin to think of Violet as a human being. I'll never understand her, of course— there is nothing to help me see what she was truly like, except my own heart.

Her feet were hurting. She limped a little when she first got up from the tombstone. It was fortunate, she thought, that she wasn't far from home.

Home. The mere word made her feel cold. She stopped on Belle Vista Avenue, at the point where she could first see the proud gambrel roof of the tall white house. Home—the word had such a wonderful ring to it.

She swallowed hard. It could never be home to her now, and, the more she let herself dwell on the sadness of that fact, the deeper she would sink into the pool of self-pity, until she might never surface again at all.

There was a piece of paper propped up on the kitchen table, and her heart jolted as if she'd touched an electrical line. So he had left a note.

But it was nothing at all, really, just a curt message that she was to return a telephone call, and the number. It took a moment for her to realise that it was a Los Angeles area code, and that the number itself was that of the syndicate. And even then she wasted another precious few minutes thinking about Marsh once more, and wondering if he had gone to work, or off somewhere with Kimberley instead...

But eventually she placed the call, and gave herself a lecture while she waited for it to go through. These people hold your entire future in their hands, she told herself, and you're an idiot if you don't stop thinking about Marsh Endicott right this instant and get down to business.

The young man on the other end of the line was one she had never talked to before. 'Miss Farrell,' he said. 'We've looked at the faxes of your drawings now——'

I should be holding my breath, Torey thought. My heart should be slamming with the suspense. Funny—I don't feel much of anything.

'And we like the concept very much indeed. We'll need to have you come in, of course, and talk about the directions you plan to take, and iron out any problems that our staff foresee. But we believe, once those things are settled, that we can go to contract.'

'That's wonderful,' she managed to say. The shock seemed to have paralysed her vocal cords.

'Why don't you come into the office on the first of April—that's two weeks—and bring along whatever you've got finished by then. Is that satisfactory?'

Two weeks, she thought. In two weeks I have to pack and move myself back to Los Angeles. And I'd better have a good portion of the strip done, too, so that they can see that I can work under deadline.

I'll manage it, she told herself recklessly. I can do it— look at what I did in that one night! And she added with grim humour, I'm not likely to be sleeping well for the next few weeks, anyway...

'Oh, and have you given a name to the strip?' the young executive wanted to know.

She hesitated for only an instant, and then said, softly, 'The Swingles.'

He repeated it, slowly. 'The research people will have to check it out, you know—it can't be too close to the name of another strip—but I don't belive that will be a problem. I think we can consider it named. Congratulations, Miss Farrell. We look forward to working with you.'

She put the telephone down slowly, and sat on the bench beside it for a long time, chewing her thumbnail. Suddenly it all seemed overwhelming—not the thrill of success, which was hardly the lift she had expected it to be, but the weight of everything that needed to be done all at once.

She walked through the big parlour, slowly, and thought about all the furniture that was still in the attic. She couldn't take it with her, and even if she could what on earth would she do with it all? She wondered if

Stephanie might take care of selling it for her, and then shook her head.

You're splitting hairs again, she told herself. What does it matter now if Marsh didn't exactly play fair with you? Trying to get even won't help. Be as honest as you can be, and at least you'll feel better when it's all over.

And the truth was that he had been right in the beginning; most of that furniture belonged with the house. It had never truly been Violet's, and so Torey had no more moral right to take it away from here than she had the right to strip the new wallpaper from the parlour and roll it back up again.

It was already dark when he came home. In fact, it was almost an echo of the first night that they had shared this house and had begun to share this fragment of their lives. Torey was in the kitchen, stirring listlessly at a bowl of minestrone, knowing that she should eat if she was to have a chance of keeping up with the vigorous schedule she had set herself today, when Marsh came in.

'I need to talk to you,' she began.

At the same instant, he said, 'Victoria, I——' and stopped.

The silence was overwhelming. 'At least close the door,' she suggested tiredly. 'And please—don't call me that any more.' From now on, she thought, her given name would mean only one thing to her. It would for ever more bring back the memory of this springtime rendezvous, and of a night when she had let herself believe in magic and miracles and unicorns and the power of love—all of them nothing but fairy-tales, she thought.

'I've reconsidered,' she went on. 'I'm going to sell you my half of the house, Marsh.'

He didn't answer, didn't even look at her.

'I'm not going to hold you up on the price, either. That first offer you made—the one Stan sent to me—it was very generous, all things considered.'

Still he didn't speak.

'And the furniture—I'm leaving it here.'

'That's thoughtful of you,' he said flatly. 'Suspiciously so, in fact. Violet left it to you.'

She bristled a little at that, but she said, calmly enough, 'Well, she shouldn't have.'

'And what are you going to do?' Marsh asked quietly. If there had been the slightest tremor in his voice—but there wasn't. 'I'm going back to California. The people at the syndicate liked the strip, and they want me back there soon. So, you see, I want to have the house settled as soon as I can. For one thing——' she tried to laugh '—I could use the money. It's going to take a while for the strip to——'

'Spare me. What happens to your strip doesn't make a shadow of difference to me.'

His voice was harsh, and it brought hot tears to her eyes. How can he talk to me like this? she thought. Was this a hint of the violence he had said he was capable of? He looked it, tonight.

He paced the width of the kitchen and came back to face her. 'I don't want the house, Torey.'

She was stunned. 'What——?' Who, he had asked her once, is going to buy half a house? She started breathing again. 'You can't be serious. And if you think that the price will come down more if you wait, let me assure you, I'm not *that* desperate.'

He shook his head. 'It doesn't matter what the price is,' he said grimly. 'I don't want it.'

Of course, she thought. There was Kimberley, and the new house on the outskirts of town. And after what Kimberley had seen this morning, she'd had a pretty strong hand to play when it came to negotiating a place to live. It was no wonder if Marsh's determination to have the house on Belle Vista had vanished into the mists.

Once she had asked Stan what would happen to her if Marsh didn't want the house after all. Now she knew that it didn't matter what happened to the house; all she could feel was her heart breaking.

'Then we'll list it for sale.' It felt like heresy to say the words, but there was no other choice now. 'We'll let Stephanie find us a buyer, and we'll both be free.'

There was a pause, only a second or two, but it felt like forever. Then he said, 'Fine. The sooner, the better. Do you want to call her, or shall I?'

CHAPTER ELEVEN

STEPHANIE was there in less than half an hour. She listened to them, and then she sighed and pulled a set of documents out of her briefcase and spread them out on the kitchen table. 'I'd advise you to give me an exclusive listing. That way you won't have every real estate person in town trampling through day and night.' She took a deep breath and added, 'I'm also a little more flexible than most if you should change your minds about selling it after all——'

'We're not going to change our minds,' Marsh said. It was cold, and he didn't even glance at Torey.

Torey added, 'And it won't bother me if they want to look at the place at midnight, because I won't be here.'

Stephanie looked as if she would like to throw the whole set of papers across the room. She muttered something under her breath and then said, more distinctly, 'All right, it's up to you.' She began writing down the house's selling points. 'Five bedrooms. Kitchen— well, the best word for it is "vintage", I'm afraid. Two full bathrooms——'

'Sort of,' Torey pointed out.

Stephanie sighed and made a note of it. 'Garage? It can't really be called that. But on the other hand, there's natural woodwork, stained glass, two fireplaces, ample storage space...When are you leaving, Torey?'

'Next week.' She felt, rather than saw, Marsh look at her, and went on, as calmly as she could, 'It's going to take a few days to fix my car and be sure it's ready for the trip.'

Marsh sighed, and Torey's fingers tightened on the handle of her coffee-mug. Would the pleasure of throwing it at him be worth the mess? She would have liked to scream that it wasn't her idea to stay around for a little longer. As a matter of fact, it had taken her most of the afternoon on the telephone even to find which garage had possession of the annoying vehicle—she had not wanted to call Marsh to ask. And, when the mechanic had told her everything that was wrong with the car, it had not been much comfort to realise that she could have been halfway back to California when it had decided to die. At least, if that had happened, she'd have been stranded in some anonymous motel, not sharing a roof with this silent stranger.

'Then we'll make my party on Sunday a farewell for you, too,' Stephanie said.

'Hello, spring,' Marsh said. 'And goodbye, Torey.'

Stephanie glared at him and said, gently, 'We'll all be sorry to see you go, Torey.'

But Marsh hadn't sounded sorry, Torey thought. He had sounded relieved.

She hadn't intended to go to Stephanie's party at all. She had planned to be on the road that day, and she had even asked Marsh to give her excuses to Stephanie. 'She'll understand, I'm sure,' she had said. 'But I just can't tell her myself.'

And besides, she had thought, being honest with him meant that he wouldn't have to worry about it any more, and it might make him stop watching her with that calculating look in his eyes.

But it didn't work out that way. Her car wasn't yet finished when the garage closed for the weekend, and so she was stuck in Springhill. 'You can pick it up at noon, Monday,' the mechanic promised, and Torey planned to hold him to his word. That would still give her ample time for the drive, and she could draw in motel rooms at night. Certainly conditions there would be no worse for her concentration than they were at the house on Belle Vista.

Marsh was still living in the house, but he didn't spend much time there. When she ventured to ask if he was going to officially move out he merely said that he was planning to stay till the house was sold, but that she needn't worry; he would pay her a reasonable rent. Torey didn't bother to answer that; she turned on her heel and left the room, just as the doorbell announced yet another estate agent with yet another client in tow. She let them in and went out for a walk, as had become her habit when the house was shown. It was too wearing on her nerves to stay there and risk overhearing the comments that were made now and then. Even Sterling Granville, she told herself, hadn't intended to knock down walls and strip out beautiful old mouldings!

She was spending a lot of her time taking walks; it seemed to Torey that people were trailing through in throngs. She wondered sometimes if they were honestly interested in buying the house, or just in looking at it. She suspected that Violet had been a bit reclusive, even before her final illness, and, if so, the house must have been a mystery to the whole of Springhill.

So she had given up on doing serious work in daylight hours and turned instead to getting ready to leave. By Sunday her packing was nearly done, and she was facing a long and solitary afternoon. She reminded herself that being alone wasn't always bad, because one could be lonelier still with one other person around if there was no sharing, no talking, no companionship. But it wasn't much comfort.

Marsh had told her that he was going to his parents' house for brunch, and then they would all be going on to Stephanie's party. She had been startled when he'd volunteered the information—had he been giving her one more reason to stay away? Whatever had made him tell her, the information certainly didn't make her own ham sandwich look any more appealing. She found herself nibbling at it with little interest, looking at her magazine without seeing a word, and thinking instead of Dolores, who must surely be feeling better by now, if she was entertaining again.

She owed Dolores Endicott an apology, she reminded herself, for not being able to finish the brochure. 'And a thank you for the wallpaper,' she muttered. 'She certainly treated me nicely enough, and it would be rude to leave without a word.' Perhaps tomorrow, before she left, if she could bring herself to just stop by the Endicotts' house, without an invitation and with no more excuse than that. She didn't think she could. But Dolores would be at the party...

'And why shouldn't I go to Stephanie's party?' she asked herself mulishly. She certainly wouldn't be crashing it, and she'd like to say goodbye to some of those people. If there were other ones there she didn't particularly want to see—well, sometimes you just had to swallow a bitter pill and go on. Why should she hide in a hole this last day, as if she were ashamed of herself?

There were certainly plenty of people, she realised the instant she stepped inside Stephanie's front door and handed her coat over to a volunteer doorman. In this kind of crowd, it should be no trouble at all to stay away from a few individuals—especially, she thought, if they were also trying to stay away from her.

Stan spotted her right away, and appeared at her side with a glass of something that was pale gold and frothy with bubbles. 'Champagne and orange juice,' he announced, and pressed it on her. 'It's the traditional beverage to greet the first day of spring around here. I'm glad you turned up. Marsh said you weren't coming.'

Which means he announced it with heartfelt gratitude, no doubt, Torey thought. Well, there was no sense in embarrassing them both now. 'My packing went faster than I expected.'

'It would have been a shame to miss this party. I wish you weren't leaving, you know.'

'That's sweet of you, Stan.'

He chewed thoughtfully on the corner of his moustache. 'I thought you could draw a cartoon strip anywhere,' he added. 'So why go back to California?'

She'd been watching the crowd, as unobtrusively as possible, and now she saw the back of Marsh's head near the double doors that led into the dining-room. Her heart gave its familiar tell-tale flutter and then settled back into the harsh, painful rhythm that had become all too ordinary in the last few days.

Because I can't bear to stay where he is and not truly be with him, she thought, and for a moment she thought she'd said it aloud. 'That's not the attitude you had when I first came,' she murmured. 'You seemed to think California was wonderful.'

'That was then,' he said stubbornly. 'There's a client of mine I have to talk to. I'll plan to stop over tonight to say goodbye, if it's all right.'

So she could try one more time to fend off the tough questions without quite telling lies? What would that accomplish? 'I think better not, Stan. I'll be awfully busy winding things up.' She shifted her champagne glass and held out her hand. 'Thanks for everything.'

He scowled. 'I thought you said you were done packing.'

Torey bit her tongue. Now you've done it, she told herself, and tried to keep her voice level. 'I'm just sneaking a brief break, I'm afraid.'

He went off, still frowning, and she sighed and mentally shook herself and went in search of Stephanie. A brief, polite word to my hostess, she thought, and I'm leaving, while I'm still in one piece. Why didn't it occur to me that the worst part of this day might be dealing with my friends?

She almost tripped over Dolores Endicott before she saw her; the woman was sitting on a hassock at the foot of a short flight of shallow steps that led into the drawing-room, her hands folded on the carved ivory handle of an antique walking-stick.

Trust Dolores not to have an ordinary cane, Torey thought.

Dolores slid over and patted the hassock beside her. Torey hesitated for the fraction of an instant before she sat down.

'I'm sorry to leave you in the lurch with the brochure,' she said.

'Oh, we'll manage. The planning you did will be a big help.' Dolores waved at someone across the room.

'How is your ankle?'

Dolores shrugged. 'Annoying. I'm sorry I couldn't finish the wallpaper.'

'Oh, it turned out all right.' The pause drew out to an awkward length. Finally Torey said, almost desperately, 'I don't suppose it will be there long anyway. The people who are looking at the house all seem to have ideas of modernising the parlour.'

'Well, it would have looked better if the whole room was done.' Dolores sounded a bit fretful.

Torey looked at her in astonishment. 'But it is. Do you mean you didn't send over the paper-hangers to finish it?'

'What paper-hangers? I kept thinking my ankle would get better, and then——' She stopped, but it didn't take a genius to know what she was thinking.

Then Marsh decided not to live there, and it didn't seem to matter any more, Torey finished in her mind. And as for the question of who had hired the paper-hangers—well, that didn't seem very important any more, either.

It was a long moment before Dolores finally smiled—
a formal, social smile that did not light up her eyes—
and said, 'We all wish you the best, Torey. We'll miss
you.'

And that, Torey thought, was as definite a dismissal
as she was likely to get. She smiled back and murmured
something polite and slipped away through the crowd.

It almost made her want to cry. She liked this woman—
more than that, she admired her. She would have enjoyed getting to know Dolores Endicott better.

As a daughter, perhaps? she asked herself ruefully.
What a dreamer you are, Torey Farrell!

She came within a couple of feet of Kimberley before
she realised it, and heard her say, 'I'm going to expand
the travel bureau, I think, and take on a couple of employees so I can spend more of my time——'

With Marsh, Torey thought. Well, perhaps the whole
disaster had roused Kimberley a bit, too, and made her
less likely to take Marsh for granted in the future.

And if I could bring myself to be grateful for something like that, Torey told herself, I'd be an immediate
candidate for sainthood. Instead, I'm going to be lucky
to get out of here before I start to cry.

She gave up the idea of talking to Stephanie. I'll call
her when I get to California, she thought, and thank her
then.

So she retrieved her coat and slipped out of the front
door, shivering as the cold air hit her. The calendar might
say it was spring now, but it was a dreary day, with a
low grey sky—a perfect reflection of her mood.

The sooner I get away from here, the better, Torey
thought, and added deliberately, Some day I will look
back on this whole thing and see the funny side of it,
and use it for the strip.

But her heart rebelled at the very idea.

The carnations were still beside Violet's tombstone.
They were withered and dry and faded to an unpleasant

brown. Even the ribbon was beginning to show signs of weathering. But it was not the flowers that Torey studied longest. It was the little wooden tripod precisely centred on the granite tombstone, holding a small brass bell that stirred slightly in the breeze and made the tiniest, gentlest little chime that Torey had ever heard.

A bell? But why?

The breeze grew stronger, and something stung Torey's face—she thought at first it was a tear that had crept upon her unnoticed, and then she realised that it was starting to snow. So much for spring, she thought, as she wearily pushed herself up from the stone to walk home. It, too—like unicorns and the power of love— was only an illusion.

She was carrying boxes downstairs and stacking them beside the front door when Marsh came home. 'You left the party early,' he said.

'I still have lots of things to do.' It was unemotional.

'You're leaving tomorrow?'

'As soon as my car is finished.' He was standing squarely in the middle of the hallway, blocking her path to the pile of boxes that she'd already brought down. 'Marsh, if you don't mind——' She gestured with the box of drawing supplies she was holding.

He moved then. She wished he would go away completely—why, on this last day, couldn't he have found somewhere else to go? Instead, he brushed the snow off his coat and hung it in the hall cupboard and then stood watching as she steadied a wobbly stack of boxes.

'Will you call me when you get to Los Angeles?' he asked.

His voice was so low that she wasn't certain she'd heard correctly. She turned around and looked at him in astonishment. There was something in his eyes...

A soft warmth started in the pit of her stomach and radiated outwards. Perhaps, after all, he wasn't quite so uncaring. If he was concerned about her safety on this long drive...

'Stephanie told me today she thinks there will be an offer made on the house next week,' he said, and the warmth inside Torey's heart faded, leaving only ashes that were colder than ice.

She turned back to her boxes with hands that almost trembled. 'That's good.'

'It's not the price we're asking, of course, but then we never really expected to get that.'

'I thought she'd set it awfully high, housing shortage or not.' Torey scarcely heard what she was saying. 'I'll leave it up to you, Marsh. If you think it's a fair price——'

'It's not a matter of price, exactly. She said that it was almost a violation of ethics to tell me the buyer's plans, but she thought we should know that they're going to cut it up into apartments.'

Torey swallowed hard. The beautiful, high-ceilinged rooms, the glorious space, the airy feeling as one room opened to another that was so unusual in a house of this age—break it up into small boxes? Cut one section of it off from another? I'd sooner see Kimberley's silver silk on the walls, she thought.

But she forced herself to shrug. 'It doesn't matter, does it? They'll own it—they'll have the right to do whatever they like.'

'That's quite correct.' His voice was expressionless. 'Very well, if it's a reasonable offer...'

Then we'll take it, she thought. The connection between us will be broken, and this entire nightmare will be over. You will be glad, Torey Farrell—and that's an order!

Marsh started up the stairs. If he shut himself into his room, she thought, he might not come out at all tonight. Tomorrow, he might be gone before she was up. This might be the last time she would see him.

And she didn't want it to be like this. She couldn't bear it. Surely there was some human warmth left somewhere between them. Surely when two people had shared both laughter and passion, as she and Marsh had done, they could break through this bone-chilling cold somehow and part, perhaps not as friends—that would be asking too much—but at least not as enemies, either. Or as strangers, which was somehow even worse.

'Marsh——' It was almost hoarse.

He stopped, but he didn't even turn around.

'I hope you and Kimberley will be very happy,' she said. It was so soft it was almost a whisper.

'Kimberley will be, I'm sure.' His tone was almost formal. 'As for me—I'll manage. Being happy is mostly a matter of making up your mind to be, I've found.'

She was stunned for a moment. 'If you're having that kind of doubt, Marsh——' The words seemed to spill out, born of her concern for him, without conscious thought, before she managed to stop herself.

'Don't stop there, Torey,' he invited. 'You seem to have the answers for everything—what do you suggest for me?'

The words seemed to tear little pieces from her heart. 'Then you shouldn't marry her.' She whispered it.

'But what do you advise me to do instead?' He came down the stairs, slowly. 'Mourn for you—is that what you're suggesting?'

She turned away with a hopeless little gesture. 'Please, Marsh, don't do this——'

'You asked for it, Victoria. You can't just run away and pretend that you didn't cause any damage here.'

'I see,' Torey said quietly. 'She's not going to marry you after all, is that it?'

'That's one way of putting it.'

'Well, that's your own fault,' she flashed. 'I didn't exactly try to seduce you.'

'That's the problem, Torey. You didn't even have to try—it's in your nature.' He was almost beside her then, close enough to raise his hand and push a lock of blonde hair back from her face. She trembled and tried to move away from him. 'No,' he said. He caught her wrist and held her firmly beside him. 'You wanted to hear this, and now you're going to stand here and listen to it. A proper pound of flesh——'

'Marsh, I'm sorry,' she said. 'Maybe Kimberley will change her mind. Give her some time to get over it. When I've been gone a while...' But her heart was saying, He's not going to marry her. He's not——

'You're desperate, aren't you?' he said almost gently. 'You're so anxious to get away from me that you don't even know what you're saying. A minute ago you told me that if I had doubts, I shouldn't marry her. Now——'

She shook her head. 'I can't think straight.'

'Join the crowd.' He let her wrist slip from his grasp and looked down at her almost quizzically. 'At first I thought my confusion was just the kind of jitters every man feels about settling down. But even before you came into it, I wondered sometimes about why it didn't bother me more to be patient about setting a wedding date— and about some other things, too. Kimberley didn't much like to be kissed...'

She's a fool, Torey thought. But then, she had always known that. 'Please, Marsh, if you must dissect this relationship, can't you find someone else to talk to? I'm hardly——'

He ignored the interruption. 'Then you popped into town like a windstorm, and without even trying you started to shake up every idea I'd ever had. Every time you mentioned Kimberley's name it jolted me.'

'Marsh, I really don't want to hear——'

'Because I would suddenly realise that I'd forgotten all about her for a while. She was the woman I supposedly loved, but not only didn't I miss her, sometimes I hadn't given her a thought in days. I told myself it was just because you were such an annoyance, but the night she got back to town, and stopped by the house, and I saw you together...'

Torey remembered that night—Kimberley in her elegant travel suit with her perfect hair and make-up, and herself, half dressed and totally dishevelled, running down the stairs to answer the door...

He said heavily, 'That's when I knew that I was engaged to the wrong woman.'

She stared at him for a long moment, and remembered the way he had looked at Kimberley that evening. Torey had thought it was adoration. Was it possible that it had been something more like shock instead? And did he mean—*could* he mean what she hoped he did?

'You could have told me,' she said. It came out sounding almost cross.

'Told you what? That I'd been such a fool that I'd almost married that frigid female? That at the same time I'd been getting over her I'd been busily falling in love with you, and I wasn't even smart enough to know it?'

Her throat had closed up. He sighed and rubbed at his temples as if his head hurt, and he didn't see the dawning wonder in her eyes.

'You'd have had a good laugh out of it, I'm sure, and that's not exactly soothing to a man's ego. I was walking a tightrope by then—I knew I had to get rid of Kimberley just as quickly as I could, without exactly jilting her.'

'Let me guess.' It was only a murmur. 'Your mother raised you to be a gentleman.'

'Well, she did.' He sounded defensive. 'And your damned stunt with the wallpaper almost ruined everything.'

'It wasn't me!' The protest was automatic.

'All right, I'll concede that Mother was to blame, too. She should have listened to her own lectures.' He shook his head. 'And heaven knows it was only wishful thinking that made me hope you wanted to break up my engagement.'

She was thinking, Then it must have been Marsh who sent the paper-hangers that day. He was the one who wanted the job done. If a parlour full of flowers was what I wanted, then he wanted me to have it.

'That's why you were so rigid about the house,' Torey mused. 'I couldn't figure out why you wouldn't even consider giving it up then, when later you couldn't wait to get rid of it.'

'It would have been a perfect home for us, Torey,' he said simply. 'You and me.'

It had the ring of truth, and also of sad renunciation. She almost gasped in fear. If he had thought that just a few days ago, what had happened to change his mind now?

'I was trying so hard to be careful,' he said. 'I knew I had to take my time with you, and hope that you would eventually realise, as I had, that we could have something very special together. I didn't want to frighten you, or to push you into something you weren't ready for. That night we went up to the Sentinel Oak—you don't know what it cost me to keep my self-control, and not to tell you everything and hope that you would understand that I really did know my own heart. I was afraid even to let myself kiss you goodnight when we got home.'

She put her hands to her head. If only he had told me, she thought. If only I had been honest with him.

'It reached the point where I didn't have any self-control left. When you went to bed with me, I was scared of what was happening, Torey, but I still couldn't stop myself. I wanted you so badly that I tried to make myself believe it would be all right. I told myself that you couldn't respond to me that way if I didn't mean something to you——'

'And then Kimberley turned up.'

'Straight out of a classic nightmare,' he said bitterly. 'And everything fell apart. It was only a casual thing, you said—a mistake, and you were sorry for it. And when you grabbed at the excuse to leave——'

'Not an excuse, exactly. I have to go to Los Angeles, Marsh.'

'I know,' he said quietly. 'But you don't have to stay there, do you?' It was not really a question.

She shook her head. 'Marsh, I——'

'I suppose I should thank you for not telling everyone the real reason you're going.'

He was going to walk away from her; she could almost feel him withdrawing already. I have one chance, she told herself. Only one...

'The real reason?' she repeated slowly, carefully. 'Do you mean the fact that I was willing to run anywhere rather than have to see the man I loved marry someone else?'

If he had suddenly been turned to stone he couldn't have been more still.

'You were being so careful to give me time,' she said softly. 'And that was the one thing I didn't need, you see, because all it did was give me the chance to think about how difficult it would be if I had to live without you.'

He moved then, dragging her into his arms without gentleness, holding her breathlessly close. His lips touched hers softly once, and then—as if the contact had set a flame to a fuse—his mouth became hard and fierce and almost pillaging, demanding a response that she gave willingly, without a hint of hesitation. That silent, trusting answer seemed the only one he needed, and he buried his face against her hair and held her as if he would never let go.

Eventually he pulled her down beside him on the couch, his hand still possessively resting on the nape of her neck.

She put her head down against his shoulder and wept a little, and when he looked at her with something that was almost fear she shook her head and tried to laugh. 'It's just that we came so close to disaster, because of our pride——'

'Pride? I've had this argument with myself a hundred times in the last four days—whether it would make any difference to tell you what I felt, whether I'd just end up looking like a fool, with you laughing at me.'

She curled up as close to him as she could. 'I'm not laughing,' she whispered. 'I'm terrified of what almost happened.'

He shook his head. 'Victoria,' he said, 'I could not have let you go without saying this. No matter how stupid it sounded or how badly it turned out.'

She couldn't even talk then. She just held him as tightly as she could.

'You see, I don't think I have any pride left where you're concerned,' he said. 'There wasn't much of anything I wouldn't try.'

'I should have realised how subtle you can be,' she murmured. 'The daffodils—not cut flowers that would fade, but bulbs that will live on.'

He smiled.

The mention of flowers made something else stir in the back of her mind. 'And carnations on Violet's grave, too.'

He shrugged. 'That was when things were going well. Sort of a peace offering—a thank-you to her for bringing you here. And then later when everything went to pieces——'

'The bell?' she guessed. 'But why?'

'It's an old folk custom to keep the evil spirits safely underground,' he confessed. 'I told you I was desperate! But it was you who put it in my mind, actually, talking about her ghost running around the house.'

Torey smiled a little. 'In that case, perhaps we'd better get started on your six kids soon, just to keep her under control.'

He kissed her, a long and deep and satisfying caress, and by the time he raised his head she was almost the consistency of butter on a summer afternoon. 'That would be no hardship for me. That first night you kissed me——'

'Wait a minute,' she said, a little breathlessly. 'Who kissed who?'

'And you fell off the couch—I wanted to come down on the floor with you and make love to you till every cell in your body screamed for mercy. But then you looked at me as if you were terrified of me——'

'I was afraid of myself,' Torey admitted. 'Afraid of caring about a man who could be so unfaithful to the woman he loved.'

'I was being very faithful to you, Victoria,' he said softly. 'Can you believe me?'

'That you really know what you're doing this time?' She pulled back and looked at him thoughtfully. 'Are there any other confessions you'd like to make?'

'My birthday isn't till May,' he said promptly.

'Why, you——'

'It was too good an opportunity to miss, even if it did bother my conscience a bit. But that's all—I've got a clean slate now. So will you marry me soon? If we're going to have all those kids...'

'Perhaps it would be better if I just lived with you for a while and got to know you.'

'Next week,' he said firmly. 'I already know everything I need to about you, and it will take the rest of my life to explore the rest.'

'Marsh, I'm shocked at you.'

'All right, then. This week. You did tell me once that you don't believe in long engagements.'

She raised her eyebrows at that and then frowned a little. 'Marsh—wouldn't it be insulting Kimberley, to be in such a rush?'

He smiled at her so tenderly that her toes started to curl in anticipation. 'Don't worry about Kimberley. She's a lot tougher than anyone gives her credit for being. Besides, by the time she left here that last morning she was extremely grateful to me for showing her what life with me would be like—too grateful, I think, even to talk about what she'd seen. I think she's been celebrating her freedom ever since.'

'Oh. Is that why you were trying to reason with her? Well, if you're sure——'

'We'll fly to Los Angeles and have a mini-honeymoon along with your business trip, and later——' But he stopped there, and went back to kissing her instead. A couple of minutes went by before he seemed to recall what he'd been saying. 'Then we'll come home to our house——'

Her eyes snapped open. 'Marsh—the house is for sale!' She looked up at him with consternation. 'We can't back out of it, either. Stephanie was right; we should have given her an exclusive——'

'We'll work it out. You said that if you could live anywhere at all . . .'

She sighed. 'You want the truth, I suppose? All right— it would be with you, wherever that happened to be.'

'That's handy,' he murmured.

'But I'd still like an old house, please, and next time you aren't going to get by with taking out antique bathtubs and——'

'Did that bother you? It'll be back next week. There's a place that restores stuff like that.' He rubbed his chin thoughtfully against the top of her head. 'Do you feel cold?'

She gasped a little and said, truthfully, 'Not when your hands are——'

'Use your imagination, Torey,' he said sternly. 'I think, myself, that it's quite unpleasantly cold in this room. In all honesty, I think we'll have to tell prospective buyers that the furnace has been acting up.'

'I see. And I suppose the roof leaks a bit, too?'

'And the foundation is probably settling. I've got it. Why don't you draw some artistic cracks on the basement walls? It could be your last commercial art job.'

She ran her fingers through his hair, delighting in the freedom to touch him, and pulled him down to her. 'We'll talk about it later,' she said firmly. 'Now, weren't you saying something about making every cell of my body scream for mercy?'

So he smiled at her and set about proving that he could.

A Free Mills & Boon Romance for you!

At Mills & Boon we always do our best to ensure that our books are just what you want to read. To do this we need your help! Please spare a few minutes to answer the questions below and overleaf and, as a special thank you, we will send you a FREE Mills & Boon Romance when you return your completed questionnaire.

We'd like to find out about your holiday habits and holiday reading, so that we can continue to provide you with the high quality Romances you have come to expect.

Don't forget to fill in your name and address so we know where to send your FREE BOOK.

Please tick the appropriate boxes to indicate your answers. ☑

1 **How many hoildays do you have a year?**

None ❑   1 ❑   2 ❑   3 ❑   More than 3 ❑

2 **Have you been on holiday within the last year?**   Yes ❑   No ❑

3 **If YES where did you go?** _____

4 **When taking holidays do you normally go?** (tick only one)

(a) Europe ❑   (b) U.K. ❑
(c) Outside Europe ❑   (d) Other _____

Please complete overleaf

5 | How do you usually travel to your holiday destination? (tick only one)

(a) Coach ❑   (b) Train ❑   (c) Plane ❑
(d) Boat ❑   (e) Car ❑

6 | What type of holiday do you usually have while you are away?

(a) Coach ❑   (b) Caravan ❑   (c) Hotel ❑
(d) Holiday Camp ❑   (e) Bed and Breakfast ❑   (f) Villa ❑
(g) Other_____

7 | Do you usually take a Mills & Boon Romance with you?   Yes ❑   No ❑

(a) If YES, How many?   1 ❑   2-4 ❑   4+ ❑
(b) If NO - Do you take any other books?   Yes ❑   No ❑

Type of book e.g. mystery, biography.

_____

8 | Do you buy books while you are away?   Yes ❑   No ❑

9 | Which age group are you in?

Under 25 ❑   25-34 ❑
35-54 ❑   55-65 ❑

Over 65 please state_____

10 | Are you a Reader Service subscriber?

Yes ❑   No ❑

If YES Sub No.

_____

Thank you for your help. We hope that you enjoy your FREE book.

Post this page TODAY TO: Mills & Boon Reader Survey FREEPOST, P.O. Box 236, Croydon CR9 9EL.   (No stamp required)

Mrs/Ms/Miss/Mr_____   EDQ4

Address_____

_____

_____

_____ Postcode _____